SKYLIGHT

A Richard Jackson Book

SKYLIGHT

JACK DRISCOLL

Orchard Books   New York

Copyright © 1991 by Jack Driscoll

Orchard Books
387 Park Avenue South, New York, NY 10016

Manufactured in the United States of America
Book design by Mina Greenstein
The text of this book is set in 11 point Electra.
1 2 3 4 5 6 7 8 9 10

Library of Congress Cataloging-in-Publication Data
Driscoll, Jack, date.
Skylight : a novel / by Jack Driscoll.
p.   cm.
Summary: Although his father expects him to attend the
University of Michigan, Buddy enrolls at Amherst to be near
his older and very wealthy girlfriend.
ISBN 0-531-05961-8
ISBN 0-531-08561-9 (lib. bdg.)
[1. Fathers and sons—Fiction.]   I. Title.
PZ7.D7878Sk   1991
[Fic]—dc20   91-10593

For my nephews,
David, Peter, and John,
and for my niece, Brie

PRELUDE

"Believe me, Buddy," my father said, "We'll do fine here. It's not like the farm—I know that—but it's a real decent place."

It wasn't, though, not at first, not for my father, who had never rented from anyone in his whole life. But I liked it a lot in the early days.

The house, a white two story, red asphalt shingles on the roof, had two dormers above the second floor where the attic was, and a huge front porch, two porches actually, one on top of the other, facing Orchard Street, where my father had parked the station wagon, as though he intended to talk to me before we ventured inside together for the first time. But he said nothing more, and I listened instead to the hard splash of the sprinkler every thirty seconds or so against the picture window, and I imagined standing inside, right behind the blurry glass, the awning down, watching myself and my father, two strangers staring back as though from the other side of a sudden rain. I knew nobody lived in there, and that my father, who had a key, would try to keep me from every room that wasn't ours, which meant the entire first floor, the ghost floor as I'd later refer to it to Phoebe Crouch, who, by that time, was my girlfriend.

My father had rented the upstairs apartment from Hazel Schwartz, a widow who was much older than he. Less than two weeks after her husband Manny's death, an aneurysm in his sleep, Hazel had locked the front door behind her and hadn't set foot in the house since.

We walked around back, and my father pointed above the garage door where he thought we could attach a basketball hoop and a backboard, but he could see I was more interested in Hazel's apartment, which he said he'd show me to satisfy my curiosity, but he didn't want me going down there alone, ever.

"Does it smell like death?" I asked, and my father laughed and said, "No, it doesn't—of course not." He said it just wasn't the cheeriest place in the world—curtains drawn, the closets full of old clothes and shoes lined up in neat rows and neckties bunched on a hook on the inside of one of the bedroom doors. And he said there were doilies on the arms of fat chairs and on the sofa ends, which made the place seem ancient, and instead of a God Bless Our Home crocheted and framed behind glass, there was this question, printed out in Magic Marker and taped to the wall above the kitchen table, Where is always? My father said that people grieving often said and did oddball things, but I didn't think the question odd at all.

We carried nothing with us into the house. Dad had been over with the last load earlier that morning. He had done all the moving by himself, helped out just one afternoon with the heavy stuff by Paul Cutney, Jr., who used to work weekends sometimes for my father in the fall when he'd butcher the hogs. He did not want the apartment empty the first time I saw it. He wanted it to look like home. But even before going upstairs, my father opened the door to Hazel's and we stepped in. She had knocked twenty-five dollars per month off the rent and had told him that he could use the washer and dryer in the pantry if he'd keep an eye on the place, be kind of a caretaker, both inside and out, and he had said yes. But I could tell right off he felt uncomfortable, as though she or Manny might appear from another room, and I knew right then that he'd keep things up in the yard—grass mowed, hedges trimmed, geraniums watered—but that he'd feel funny even coughing down here or clearing his throat or turning on the TV while he waited for the laundry to finish.

I felt comfortable immediately and I pushed open a door and stepped into a library—what seemed like thousands of books on the shelves covering the walls. Dad peeked in behind me and, when I looked up at him, he seemed confused, like how could anyone ever read this much or even want to?

"Come on," he said. "Buddy, shut the door. I don't want you in here."

I nodded okay and walked across the living room to where the baby grand was, the bone white keys shining in the darkness. I sat down on the black bench and, after raising it to its full height by twisting those two knobs on the sides, I smiled over at my father and, with my index finger, I hit a C, which was badly out of tune. Although the piano top was closed, that single flat note seemed much too loud, and louder still as we both listened to it a second time and then a third until my father said, "Stop. Stop it."

Without even looking up, I waited a couple of seconds and then I shut the shiny lid to the keyboard, shutting it, I thought, on those few words of his, and he knew it and said, "Let's go upstairs now." But I didn't want to and I stood up and stared at all the photographs, about ten or fifteen, clustered in stand-up frames on the piano top—old ones, wedding portraits mostly, and no shots of children or grandchildren, every image in sepia.

My father kept no albums around the house, and years ago he had put away all pictures of my mother, boxed them, wrapped those behind glass with towels to protect them in storage. Whenever I would ask to see them, he'd say, "Please, Buddy, I can't. Not yet, not right now," meaning, I later learned, not ever. But he always carried a snapshot of her in his wallet, and some nights when I couldn't sleep, I'd sneak into his bedroom and I'd take the wallet from the back pocket of his pants and I'd silently shut the door behind me. Outside on the back porch I'd slide the snapshot from behind the crinkled plastic, and I'd light a candle and tilt the photograph back and forth, back and forth until the reflection of that small flame danced across the glossy emulsion of her cheeks, her lips, those wide, dark eyes that resembled mine, and I'd believe then that she was alive, breathing in front of me, and missing her, I'd start to cry.

I thought of that when I picked up an eight by ten, of Hazel, I imagined, sitting on a white horse, crop in her left hand, a velvet riding helmet on, but she was holding the reins much too tightly so that the horse's teeth were showing, its lips curled back. The horse was sweating badly too. Hazel looked uncomfortable up there, frightened even, and I don't know why, but I wondered if it was Hazel who'd found Manny dead, and if not, exactly where she had been sitting or standing, in what room and at what time, when she heard about her husband's death, where I'd be when my father died, and if I'd frame the only photograph I had of him, standing in front of the barn. And where would I hang or lean it?

I was about to say to my father, "She's very pretty," but he spoke first, almost in a whisper. He said, "Don't pick up anything else down here," and he took the photograph from me and walked to the nearest window, and in that sliver of sunlight along the edge of the dark green shade, he stared at the picture of Hazel, then back at me, and he said for the second time, "You're never to come down here alone."

"I know," I said, and before handing the photograph back to me he wiped it with his sleeve. "Put it back where it was," he said, and he turned away then and headed through the arched doorway into the kitchen, where the stairs were, and I hurried to catch up, knowing I'd disobey and sneak back down after we got settled, and I'd explore each room thoroughly. And maybe I'd really become that imaginary self I saw behind the watery glass when we first drove up, a kind of phantom lookout who already felt safe in this abandoned apartment, all alone among the crazy landlady's ghosts.

O N E

Phoebe Crouch lived a good half hour away, her family's house overlooking Glen Lake, where the rich people from Chicago and Detroit summered. I had met her at a dance when I was fifteen, four years after moving into town. She told me that first night that her father owned huge parcels of land all around there, thousands and thousands of acres, hoping someday, as a retirement project, to develop a village of condos, a ski resort, and a golf course that would help put northern Michigan on the map, bolster its failing economy. My father called it country club expansion, and once, tugging the bill of his Blue Seal Feeds cap, he said that as a rule of thumb we should shoot speculators on sight. But he looked at me then and smiled, and I knew there was no real danger of his ever doing that. He was just angry about how so many of the small farms were vanishing, how real estate investors, gazing across a field of corn or string beans or potatoes, saw it only as a potential par five.

So I didn't say too much to him about Mr. Crouch, except that he was rich. Following directions Phoebe had given me over the phone, I instructed my father to drop me at the Crouches' front gate, elaborate ironwork, something more suited to Grosse Pointe or Newport, Rhode Island. The gate was wide open, but my father would not drive through, staring instead from one thick glass owl to the other, each perched wide-eyed on its separate brick pillar, as if guarding the grounds in the half-light. Inside each of their chests a tiny red bulb pulsed like a heart.

I did not get out of the car until my father said, "Call when you're ready," and then he waited a minute as though I might be ready now, holding a bouquet of lilacs at the entrance to this foreign and very expensive landscape. My father had snipped them from the huge lavender and white bushes in Hazel's backyard, tied the stems together with a piece of white twine, and handing the bunch to me said, "Always introduce yourself with a gift—flowers or oranges or a half-dozen ears of corn—something your life is known by. Show up empty, and they'll think you're rich. From then on you'll be lying to keep pace."

When he finally drove away, I started down the long driveway, which sloped through terraces of imported shrubs and small clusters of dwarf trees: plum and crab apple and dogwood, the new petals so white above the soft, black peat moss. Somewhere close by I imagined a footbridge, and below in the calm pool, Phoebe's reflection, two goldfish rising from behind her eyes to nibble the surface with their gentle lips. At that moment this new world appeared clear and accessible, and my father's cockeyed scheme of so common a present could ruin my chances of getting in. Before reaching the house, I tossed the lilacs away, the sweet scent hanging a few long seconds in the air. When the scent cleared, even though there was a doorbell, I lifted the heavy brass knocker and let it fall.

I hoped Phoebe would answer the door and escort me into the spaciousness of this multilevel, solar-heated house of cedar, the kind I'd seen featured in *Better Homes and Gardens* when I breezed through the magazine once or twice in the waiting room outside the dentist's office.

Mr. Crouch was an architect and inventor and he had spared no mental or material expense creating this one-only custom home. But what he was most proud of was a planetarium he'd designed some years back for downtown Detroit, the blueprint later enlarged to cover an entire wall of his living room. Phoebe had told me that sometimes, using a wooden pointer, he'd take you on a tour, slowly closing his eyes as though he were hypnotized, his head tilted back. Then he'd describe each constellation, his voice growing softer and softer until it drifted into the pure and untraceable silence of the universe. Phoebe's mom would crack a wide, confident smile, then squeeze her hands together in exuberant adoration and lead him by one elbow, as though he were blind, into another room, to the couch where he'd continue on with his dreaming through even more distant galaxies.

The planetarium was never constructed. "The city's loss," he had responded simply one night at dinner. But he designed an observatory and had it built on the hill out back, just a hundred yards from the house. He named the observatory Beyond. "And beyond and beyond and beyond," he'd say, but nobody else ever called it that. I didn't know why, but I felt that before I left that night to go home I would kiss Phoebe there, pretending to know something about the powerful attraction new lovers feel under the stars.

When nobody answered, I tried the bell. It did not ring the way cheap bells do to a second floor or to the apartments in a tenement building where a visitor waits with his hand on the doorknob until the lock is buzzed free from upstairs.

The Crouches' bell played the first six or seven notes of "The Star-Spangled Banner," the deep bass tones echoing throughout the house. Phoebe explained that her father was not really patriotic, and that during election years he'd change the music to the Canadian national anthem, ring the bell a few times, and announce, "That's a country I like!" He was full of those kinds of utterances, absolutely clear about what he liked or didn't.

The door opened finally, and Mr. Crouch just stood there staring, not saying "Hi" or "Come in" or "Glad to meet you." He was silent, his dark eyes dilating slowly into focus as though I had awakened him from a long sleep. After a minute he stepped out of his shoes and walked away, leaving them, I guessed, for the next time he was called on to greet the company. Each shoe had a V cut out of the back, and I thought it must be because of corns or calluses or plantar's warts. But Phoebe later said nope—her father had modified a whole closetful of expensive footwear, new oxfords and white bucks and wing tips, completing each careful alteration with a mat knife, then tying a double knot after he'd soaked the leather laces in water, making sure they would never come loose. "Why?" I had asked her, and she'd repeated word for word what Mr. Crouch had said: "Someone got wealthy on the shoehorn. On the Slinky, on the Hula Hoop. You'll remember that if you cut the backs out of your shoes."

He was a man of lessons and riddles, though he spoke seldom and rarely managed a complete thought, drifting, I supposed, into the mathematics of improbable angles that might someday balance the weight of the world. But I was not as much interested in cosmic theories as I was in the shape of Phoebe's small breasts, so firm under her white blouse as she arrived to rescue me, abandoned and confused at the empty doorway, a little scared and almost ready to leave.

Phoebe said, "You're on time," as though that were un-usual, and then she took my hand and said, "Well, don't just stand out there. Come on in."

Bissell, Phoebe's younger brother, came bounding down the hall. Any other house I'd ever been in would have shaken under his awkward, lumbering stride. But the dense natural wood and thick carpeting seemed to absorb all vibration, as though Bissell had floated toward us light-footed from a dream. He was only ten, but already he was bigger than me, and if there was any truth about growing into one's feet, Bissell Crouch would fill out around six feet five inches and 260, an offensive guard or tackle on the high school football team. I nodded hello and he said, "Say 'toy boat' as fast as you can, five times." I tried, but on the third repetition it sounded like "toy boyt." Bissell erupted with laughter, spun in a circle on the balls of his huge feet, and catching his balance against the wall said, "I knew it, 'toy boyt.' " And he started to hiccup, laughing harder and harder each time "boyt" jumped a few octaves in his throat.

Phoebe, annoyed, said, "Bissell, get a drink of water and get out of here!" He returned a minute later from the kitchen, holding a white mug. Taking a long gulp, he lowered his head forward, pinched his nose closed, and swallowed hard. Phoebe explained that every time he got excited he got the hiccups, which meant every time he tried out a tongue twister on her friends. If they refused to play, he'd bet them a quarter they couldn't say one without slipping up, and if they won he'd refuse to pay, accusing them of cheating, of being too deliberate and stuck-up. And he'd disappear into his bed-room. His favorite tongue twisters were the ones that caught you in a swear, and those he'd try over and over on himself, sometimes into his portable tape recorder, introducing each tongue twister as he might the title of a poem, articulate and slow:

"I Slit a Sheet and a Sheet I Slit."

Then, as if changing speeds, he'd let fly, the syllables colliding so that what came out had a mind of its own. It made absolutely no difference to Bissell which way the swears arrived, but just before they did he'd crank up the volume as he hid behind chairs and drapes in different rooms. Phoebe's friends would say, "Your brother is disgusting, a little twerp," but Bissell would shout at them, "I'm rubber— you're glue. Everything you say bounces off me and sticks to you." Then he'd laugh and hiccup all the harder.

I followed Phoebe into the dining room. Tapping the back of a chair, she said to me, "Right here," and she left to help out in the kitchen. Mr. Crouch was already sitting down, not at the head of the table, but directly across from me. He kept studying a blueprint as if it were the evening paper, and he did not glance up when Phoebe returned, followed by her mother, a pale and nervous woman who, despite her college-girl clothes, seemed much too old for her children.

Phoebe introduced me, and I nodded and reached out my hand. Mrs. Crouch said, "Oh," not so much in surprise that I was really there, but as a strategic pause before explaining she couldn't shake hands. "I'm handling food," she said, enunciating each word as she might for someone reading lips. From the kitchen I could smell and hear steaks sizzling under the broiler.

"Phoebe tells me you grew up on the farm."

"The" made the farm seem Southern and backward.

"Where they processed their own meat from steers," Phoebe added, confusing what I had told her.

"In the fall," I said. "But mostly it was hogs. We sold bacon and sausage."

Looking up for the first time, Mr. Crouch dismissed the romance of local harvest: "There are more people killed each year by farmyard hogs than by sharks," he announced. "Remember that if you're selling property along the Florida coast."

For a minute Mrs. Crouch seemed to examine me more closely, as if searching for scars or a missing finger. Her husband's perceptions were hers exactly, though she didn't know it until he spoke. Then she agreed completely, sometimes repeating what he'd just said as if for emphasis, nailing down the final word. When the timer on the stove signaled her back to the kitchen, she handed me a bottle of wine and a corkscrew, nodding her head as if accepting a dance, and said, "Do me the honor, will you?" and left me to fill the only three glasses on the table, one of them being mine, the stem long and elegant, the red filling the oval bowl on top like a rose.

There was no prayer, though Mr. Crouch had his head bowed and lifted his chin just enough for his wife to tie a bib around his neck. They had saved the bib, a souvenir from a trip to Cape Cod, and used it now for every dinner, surf or turf. "It's a good idea," he said, "like wearing a life preserver while driving across the Mackinac Bridge." It made perfect sense to his wife, who explained the lesson in one word: "Precaution," she lectured, and sat down. Bissell, right next to me, was rocking on the back legs of his chair, and across from him Phoebe held the plates while her mother, at the head of the table, served the meat, already sliced, thin and rare, the juices collecting in a pool where the small channels of the cutting board funneled together. Phoebe spooned on the gravy, then passed the plate along. Baked potatoes followed, then a basket of rolls, steamed asparagus on a white platter. In the center of the table was a huge wooden salad bowl, the tossed greens shiny under the flames of the candles.

Bissell reached out with a battery-powered back scratcher, the kind with a plastic hand at the end of a thin, metal arm. He balanced a single wedge of tomato in its tiny blue palm and, guiding it over his plate, he switched on the power, the tomato vibrating off into his glass of milk. He cracked up, as hard as he had from the tongue twister, and Phoebe, in singsong reprimand, began: "Oh, Bissell!" As she hung on the double *ll*'s, her mother joined in: "Oh, Bissell," followed by Mr. Crouch in a deeper, more resonant tone, as though they were singing a round of "Row, Row, Row Your Boat."

It did no good. Mocking the ridiculousness of this family trio, Bissell sang back, "Oh, Phoebe, oh, Mom and Dad," and Phoebe responded, angry this time, "Bissell, you're incorrigible."

But I thought it was simpler than that. Bissell Crouch was a heathen, and I liked him for dispensing with the awkward mannerisms of the rich and cultured. Next to him I felt almost refined, more confident now that I'd tasted my first dry sip of wine.

"To your wealth," I announced, meaning to say "health," and Mr. Crouch came suddenly alive from behind the shield of his blueprint, not to interject a riddle this time, but to lean forward to touch glasses in slow and perfect agreement.

After dinner Mrs. Crouch cleared the dishes, and Mr.

Crouch, passing the wall phone just as it rang, lifted the receiver and, without answering, simply dropped it to the floor. Phoebe was there in a few seconds to say hello. It was for Bissell, who took the call in the privacy of another room.

Phoebe waited until she heard Bissell's voice on the other line, and she hung up. Corking what was left of the wine, she handed me the bottle and led me, a little drunk, to the observatory, an octagon on stilts. It was built on the side of the hill that overlooked an expanse of woods and meadow and, winding through in a long, slow S, the narrow yet deep Black Creek I would fish in the coming summer months. But right now the earth was dark, and all I could see through the huge windows and skylight were shapes of clouds passing the full moon, and in the corner of the room, the length of the double cot Phoebe illuminated with her flashlight. "Sometimes my father naps here in the afternoons," she explained, and I knew then I needed no planetary maps for such simple and obvious navigation. What I didn't know was what to do after I lay down on the cot, my head spinning on the cool pillow. It helped when I closed my eyes, thinking how the closest stars were millions and millions of miles away. Phoebe called me back, whispering, "Don't fall asleep. If you do, I'll put my blouse back on and call for your ride." Then she straddled me and gently lifted both my hands and rubbed my fingertips on the undersides of her breasts. I needed nothing else to sober me up, and when the sudden moonlight flooded the room, I drew her toward me into the shadow of the huge telescope tilted above the valley, so silver now to anyone observing with the naked eye. But I had focused on something more dazzling—Phoebe's body beginning to move in a slow circle, the tiniest orbit that was ever the world.

An hour later, when my father met me at the top of the driveway, he asked, "How'd the lilacs work?"

"There's nothing they really want," I said, trying only to invent an excuse for not bringing such cheap flowers another time, just to throw them away.

"Is that right?" he asked, stepping hard on the gas, as though desperate to get away.

T W O

That fall and winter it was hard finding time to spend with Phoebe. She was attending St. Catherine's, a private girls' school, and she never got home before 5:00 P.M. We talked on the phone a lot, sometimes for over an hour. My father was working the 3:00 P.M. to 11:00 P.M. shift at the Fisk, the tire plant outside of town, so he couldn't drop me off at the Crouches'. I'd see Phoebe most weekends, which wasn't enough, so it felt good to see spring arrive and, in early June, for school to end. I was glad to get out of the house more often, away from my father, who each morning at breakfast garnished every conversation with hints about me getting a job. But I didn't give two hoots about that, busing tables or pumping gas or stocking auto parts in some warehouse for minimum wage. So I spent as much time at the Crouches' as I could, not a boarder exactly, but I'd bunk in the observatory as many as three or four nights a week. Phoebe would sneak up, and we'd set the alarm clock, and she'd be back in her own bed before first light. Her parents must have known—they had to know—but they never said a thing. It was as though Phoebe and I were already engaged, and Mr. Crouch even offered us the Lincoln Continental one evening to go see *Dr. No* at the Victory. I didn't feel at all funny when he handed me the keys, then money for the tickets and for popcorn.

I had never even been in a car that expensive. I adjusted the power seats and settled back a minute and breathed the deep redolence of genuine leather. Then Phoebe turned on the radio and slid closer and kissed me on the lips and asked how I'd gotten so handsome. I smiled and said I didn't know and lowered the tilt steering wheel to suit me, and then I adjusted the rearview mirror before driving off in such grand style to watch James Bond.

We had invited Bissell, but he said no, and it was a good thing he hadn't come, hadn't seen all the weapons and assault contraptions in the film. Already he'd begun making bombs in the basement—thousands of match heads soaked in gasoline and stuffed into bottles and jars. He said to me one afternoon, "Come on, Buddy. Hurry up. Come on," and down by the creek he lit a short, shoelace fuse and tossed the bottle grenade style and ducked, and I did too. When the bomb exploded a few seconds later, fragments of glass sprayed burning into the water, and upward too, slashing through the silver undersides of leaves.

It was nothing for Bissell to spend an entire day scraping powder from rolls of caps, scraping and scraping just so he could ignite a fistful after dark in the backyard, plastic toy soldiers and tanks arranged so they'd be scorched, as he said, "just like in a fire storm." And he had cut out, and taped to his bedroom wall, that *Life* magazine photograph of Thich Quang Duc, the first of the Buddhist monks to burn himself to death in protest. Bissell Crouch, armed and ready, said what interested him most in the world was war.

At Bissell's age, I had liked explosives too, and my father, dynamiting stumps one September on the farm, let me detonate the charges. And I don't know where he got hold of them, but every Fourth of July he'd set off hammerheads and cherry bombs, always keeping me at a safe distance behind him, a sparkler in my hand. I liked the noise of celebration, the way I liked the sound of guns. I learned to respect and shoot them early, when I was younger than Bissell, but I was glad Mr. Crouch decided against his son's owning a .22 at eleven years old. To placate Bissell, I said I would let him practice with mine, that if he listened to me and handled the rifle carefully I might even take him squirrel hunting in the fall. He said, "No. I want a throwing knife instead."

Nobody said no to Bissell about the knife. He carried it every day in a leather sheath on his belt. Unlike my Case, Bissell's blade had no cutting edge, no polished, deep-grained wooden handle. It was a single piece of cold steel, heavy and perfectly balanced, and with a firm flip of his wrist, he could bury the wide tip in a plank of wood or in the trunk of any tree. For practice he bought dozens of brightly colored targets of deer and bear and bobcats at Upland Sports, but those he mutilated quickly, shredding the paper against the backstop of hay bales. So he improvised. From the back deck he'd come within inches of whatever he aimed at on the ground—a flip-flop kicked off, a clothespin under the line. Sometimes, during cookouts, he'd slow-glide a paper plate over the railing, and as soon as it hit the ground, he'd attempt to pin it there, as he said, "right through the heart."

Mrs. Crouch hated his doing that and one evening, after hamburgers on the grill, she asked him to stop. Phoebe said, "That's right, Bissell. Cut it out." She and I had started playing badminton without a net, just hitting the birdie way up, whacking its red rubber nose as hard as we could, sending it skyward. The birdie drifted slightly in the breeze. When my turn came, Phoebe did not move and, staring up, she did not see Bissell cock his right arm behind his ear and snap the knife down hard from the deck. But she heard it slash the ground between her bare feet, and she screamed when she saw it there, the upper blade smeared with ketchup. Mrs. Crouch said, "Dear God," and Bissell laughed and whooped and brought his fingers back and forth from his lips, shouting his war cry as Mr. Crouch, standing in the doorway behind him, watched his son in silence. Empty-handed, Bissell jumped from the top stair to retrieve his knife, and on his knees he wiped the blade clean on the thick grass.

Phoebe, crying, said, "That's not funny," and picked up the white shuttlecock as though it were a wounded dove, and then she ran inside, away from her brother, whose kid games frightened her, now that he aimed real knives, aimed close enough to maim.

To calm Phoebe down, I explained how I used to play splits at school when I was Bissell's age, out on the lawn at recess. A lot of kids did. What I didn't tell her was that we always used a dull jackknife, and we always stood facing each other, just a few feet apart, and we were careful, deliberate with every toss. I remembered then how Frank Scamehorn could stretch farther than anyone else, almost doing a complete splits, and how he was playing one lunch break with Atley McKelvey, who'd brought a new Swiss Army knife, heavy and real sharp, which changed the game. Right off Frank was losing badly, balancing himself with his left hand on the grass below his crotch. I handed him the knife in that position, and he lobbed it high, flipping it in one slow revolution, hoping it would land point first a few yards from Atley and win the game. It landed handle first, a depressing thud. We all laughed while Frank moaned, his leg muscles straining, and Atley, still standing with his feet together, wanted, like all of us, to see if Frank could stretch that extra inch. Atley cut his throw too close and bounced the new blade tip off Frank's big toe. "You dink," Frank yelled, falling backward and yanking his sneaker off by the heel, and then the white sock. The skin was blue and peeled back a little where it met the toenail, though there was no blood. He did not get up and limp over to pick up the knife and threaten Atley, who was not nearly as big or as tough. None of us fooled around that way with weapons. Atley apologized, and Frank said again, "You're really a dink sometimes, you know that? Do you?" When Atley said yes, everything was okay.

But Bissell, boastful about his accuracy, was not sorry and he ridiculed the fainthearted like Phoebe who mistrusted the masters. That throw of his, he said over and over, was a piece of cake. And he described then how circus throwers could do it blindfolded, outlining with knives the dramatic curves of a beautiful woman as crowds both screamed and cheered the dangerous flight of chrome blades spinning under the glare of spotlights. He sounded crazy—no longer just a goofy kid sounding off to get attention. He said, "I mean it. I intend to become a professional knife thrower." Mrs. Crouch swallowed and said, "Oh, Bissell, please, no, please don't even talk like that," but Mr. Crouch, understanding more than a little bit about child psychology, knew better than to discourage him outright. Instead, he went the other way, buying Bissell a complete set of knives, hoping the obsession would harmlessly run its course, as it had with a metal detector and then with a motorbike he drove every day, rain or shine, around the property for a month. Then one evening he leaned it against the back of the garage, covered it with a tarp, and never started it again.

The big questions in the Crouch household usually surfaced at dinner. We were eating spareribs, and Bissell, his face and fingers greasy, asked Phoebe if she would be his assistant.

"And do what?" Phoebe asked.

"Just close your eyes," he said, "and trust me not to miss."

Mr. Crouch, who had been following Vietnam daily in *The New York Times*, must have had that on his mind when he said, "Save it for the army, Bissell."

"I'm enlisting in the marines as soon as I'm eighteen," Bissell said, and his father, sorry he had brought up the military, responded, "We don't ever want a Crouch going anywhere he might get killed."

"And we don't want you killing me," Phoebe said, and Mrs. Crouch, bewildered by the conversation, ended it by saying, "We've never talked crazy like this before. Nobody's getting stabbed or disfigured or going to war," and she got up fast from the table, throwing her linen napkin down hard on her chair and yanking the blind fiercely shut on the sharp light that was slicing across her face through the window.

After dinner I helped Phoebe rinse and stack the dishes in the dishwasher. Had it been any darker outside, I wouldn't have seen Bissell charge, knife taped like a bayonet to his Daisy air rifle, down the hill and into the woods. Phoebe saw him too and, in the long silence between us, I half expected to see the flash from one of Bissell's homemade bombs. Instead, I saw Mrs. Crouch, in her white sweater, walking toward the spot where her son had disappeared into the woods. She called to him again and again, and I imagined her looking back at us, outlined together at the window. Phoebe, turning to me, said, "Please go after him. He listens to you."

"She's right," Mr. Crouch said, standing there behind us, and we could all hear the intermittent pop, pop of his air rifle—a sniper, I thought, and I didn't want to walk in on him, unarmed in the dark, mistaken for the enemy.

"Take the searchlight," Mr. Crouch said, as though reading my mind, but I didn't switch the beam on until I was right next to Mrs. Crouch. When I did, shining it low into the trees, there was Bissell, not twenty feet away, aiming at us, from one to the other.

"You're both dead a hundred times," he said, and Mrs. Crouch, after Bissell had passed us by on his way back to the house, took hold of my arm and squeezed it and said, "While we have our lives . . . ," but she didn't finish, confused, I guess, by having just been make-believe killed by her son when all she intended to do was save him.

T H R E E

The summer before my senior year, I hunted around for a job, something that would give me a lot of time to spend with Phoebe, who was leaving for Smith College at the beginning of September. I was the only one in town who applied for the "scumbuster" position, a misleading title for what turned out to be pretty decent employment during July and August, those months the algae settled each night on Grady's Pond, the local swimming spot for families who didn't vacation on the beaches of Lake Michigan, who didn't have the kind of money it took to rent in Northport or Leland or Glen Arbor. Grady's was cheap, and it was safe and clean and cold deep down, being spring fed. Most people didn't know the scum even existed. But it did, thick and greenish brown some mornings when I arrived at six-thirty, hours before anyone else. I suppose I could have slapped the scum away, using one of the oars from the lifeguard's rowboat, but it didn't bother me at all to dive right in and backstroke or butterfly through the shallow water, churning things up real good. Then I'd swim out beyond the enclosure of lifelines and circle the white raft a few times, kicking and splashing wild as a mute drowner.

There was a diving board attached that had powerful

spring. Sometimes I'd cannonball the scum, aiming at a certain gob, the way kids might target frog's eggs from a bridge with a good-size rock, a two hander. And still squeezing my knees to my chest, I'd drift down deeper and deeper through those cold pockets. I liked that slow-motion feeling, the particles of green light rising all around me, the way silence rises sometimes around the edges of dreams. It didn't matter how long I stayed at the pond (that was the part of the job I liked best, that and being left alone) just as long as the water surface was clean when I left. Usually that meant about an hour and a half. After that I'd be shaking pretty bad, blue lipped, goosebumps everywhere, but I'd dry off and change right there in the driver's seat of Phoebe's new MGB, the heater already cranked up full blast. Then I'd head over to join the Crouches for breakfast—eggs Benedict or croissants and bacon, melon slices, blueberry buttermilk pancakes—incongruous entrées for a scumbuster, but I was refining my tastes that final summer at home, having worked up a huge appetite for this other life, the one my father's ignorance and isolation had always stunted.

When I got hired, he said, "It isn't a lousy job, just lousy training." Not the scumbuster part—he said lots of people, good people, dirtied their hands earning an honest wage. What he objected to was a ten-hour work week, especially now that I was supposed to be saving for college. He said I could at least work part-time bagging groceries at the IGA, or pumping gas someplace, or even get some work at the Fisk, for that matter, piecework so I could really bust my butt for two months and pocket some real money. He was pretty sure he could get me in by pulling a few strings.

At first I thought piecework was an alternative to war work, and I liked that idea, but I said no anyway, needing afternoons to study, telling him the higher my SATs, the bigger my scholarship to U of M, though I had in mind to go someplace else instead, someplace a lot closer to Phoebe. He said hold on just one minute—around here, after age seventeen, everyone pulled his own weight, which did not mean I had to pay for rent or food or even for gas for the station wagon if I wanted to use it to go hunting or fishing or out on a date. It simply meant that I got to work, got started growing up.

"Don't get me wrong about school," he said, and I never did. He was the first to acknowledge college as the ticket to better things, but he'd argue that a person could be over-educated too and miss out on real life, the nuts-and-bolts stuff. He said real insight drifted unmolested in and out of a man's life no matter who he was or what he was doing: planting cabbages or replacing shingles on a barn roof or maybe just shaking off his gloves for a smoke after stretching new wire between cedar posts. The mistake scholars made was thinking they had a stranglehold on knowledge, that they could make it "give" in secret, interrogating it as though they had to break some complicated code and then interpret it for the masses, "for us," he said, "the unannounced, the remote and witless bystanders." And then he blamed what he called my work apathy on the Crouches and said, as angry as I'd heard him in a long time, that I ought to move in over there, let them adopt me and pay the damn tuition next year. "Next thing I know," he said, "you'll be following her [meaning Phoebe] off to the East Coast, to Massachusetts to rub elbows with the high-muck-a-mucks."

Though I didn't say so, that was exactly what I had in mind—to attend Amherst College, which Phoebe said was the most difficult school in the country to get into. "But in's in," she said. "Once there, well, they look after their own."

Unlike Phoebe, I had no connections, nobody in my family who had ever gone on after high school, nobody who had ever left northern Michigan for more than a few months, and then only to come racing back home. Phoebe, even with mediocre board scores and average grades, had been accepted at Smith. She was, as she had maintained against my urging her to study more, a virtual shoo-in. Both her mother and grandmother had graduated from Smith, without distinction, but with the means to contribute substantially each year to the college through the alumnae fund.

What my father contributed to was his own small-time philosophy of denial, his belief that the foundation of all survival—not happiness, never that—was staying put, enduring the seasons and setbacks, the long weeks working the graveyard shift, waiting life out no matter what it dealt you, no matter how many empty hands you were forced to play. And that's the metaphor he kept using, explaining how the Crouches' world was all bluff and he was calling it once and for all, cards on the table.

Maybe I shouldn't have said what I did then. I said, "They'll win. They'll win every game with a flush or a full house." And saying that, our apartment seemed so suddenly empty, and empty of taste and symmetry, a hodgepodge of design—not a single bookshelf, no paintings or photographs or framed posters hanging on the walls, no stereo speakers, no wine rack in the kitchen.

And my father said, resolutely and without looking around, "I've got nothing you want, do I? Not a single thing valuable enough to hand down?" He did not wait for the answer, for which I was grateful. He just got up from the table and went slowly downstairs, I guess to check the new growth on the two blue spruce he'd planted that spring in the backyard,

trees Hazel had bought and sent over from Hoeksema Nurs-
ery.

I thought how even the contents of my father's will, had
he ever bothered to write one, would be a burden, no more
than a truckload for Goodwill. But I did not feel gypped, not
anymore, certain now that I was on my way out finally,
financed only by dreams so far, dreams that seemed foreign
and worthless and unobtainable to anyone but the rich and
educated, those privileged few who were ready and anxious
to recruit me.

I'm not sure why my father agreed to have Sunday dinner at
the Crouches' the very next week, or why I even asked him,
but I did, figuring that it was not my right to decline the
invitation. When he accepted, I said, nervous and jumping
the gun, "Just meet them halfway. They're okay people.
They've always been nice to me anyway." I thought he might
interpret this as a lecture and get all riled again and start in
on his antisnob routine, asking sarcastically if it would be
acceptable for him to say "movie" instead of "film," and if
he was expected to dress up fancy in his best pants for the
occasion—excuse me, his best "slacks" or "trousers." But
there was none of that, no cynical maneuvering to drive home
that same dull point about lines and class, no belligerence
at all.

He acted tired, played out like a man who has dealt himself
a final losing hand and knows enough to fold. I felt sorry for
him and wanted, right then in the living room in front of
that black-and-white TV with "The Price Is Right" just end-
ing, to explain that I wasn't turning away or siding against
him. But all I said was, "Good, I'm glad you'll join us," and
later in bed, unable to fall asleep, I realized how "us" in any

context excluded him and always would, the outsider who'd consented to share a meal too late, as though there was still time to catch a glimpse of where I was headed, to figure out how long I might be gone.

Whenever I thought about it objectively, I had to admit the Crouch family did seem a little strange at first, a bit eccentric, but I decided not to prep my father, not even to tell him about Bissell's word games, how they drove Phoebe and Mrs. Crouch half-nuts. The newest was his intentional misuse of words that either looked or sounded alike, such as "antidote" and "anecdote," or "syntax" and "synapse," or "ornamental" and "oriental," or to use two of his favorites, "erotic" and "erratic." If it was Saturday afternoon and the Tigers were losing again on TV and someone, me or Phoebe or Mr. Crouch, just in passing, were to ask how come, what's the problem this time, Bissell would say, "The pitchers, they're all erotic." He'd say it straight-faced, his eyes never leaving the screen, and I'd imagine Frank Lary or Mickey Lolich with their flies unzipped, pretending to be holding a runner on first, but staring instead through the glove's webbing at a beautiful woman sunning in the box seats.

"The simple power of suggestion," Bissell would later preach, and I understood then the distortion caused by a single word out of place. I believed Bissell might someday, with a little discipline, become a poet; without it, a pervert prowling along the hedges of backyards with his binoculars. I told him that once, and he said, "Pervert and poet—they go together." He believed the subject of all real writing, serious writing, was the flesh. He had devoured *Portnoy's Complaint* and *Naked Lunch*, his one-two punch, by the time he was eleven years old, and he believed if the body made for good reading (the *only* reading, he'd say), then it made for good conversation too, and he was always ready to make whatever slight alterations were necessary to turn a sentence toward smut.

One I liked a lot was when Mr. Crouch, really raking over one of the firm's newest architects one night after dinner, said, "If the guy had even an inch of foresight . . . ," and Bissell, revising on the spot, repeated just slightly under his breath, "If the guy had even an inch of foreskin . . . ," and on and on like that, wild with laughter.

Sometimes he'd slur his words, asking someone a direct question, someone like the mailman or paperboy. He might say, "Tickle your ass with a feather?" Most often the person addressed would say, "What?" or "I beg your pardon," and Bissell, enunciating slowly this time and pointing outside at the rain or wind, would say, turning it to a statement, "Typically nasty weather." I figured the odds were fifty-fifty at best that my father would tolerate Bissell. If not, it could be a long evening.

I already had the car idling when Dad came down the back stairs. "I'll drive," he said, and I slid into the passenger's seat and rolled down the window. I didn't say so, but he looked real sharp, white shirt and gray flannel slacks, and I kind of wished we were on our way to dine out alone, somewhere fancier than we'd ever been, to chat and laugh and maybe get a little drunk together for the first time, the way I imagined fathers did with their sons who were attending the Ivy League colleges. I pictured places with names like Yankee Clipper or Lord Bentley Inn. I played a little with that notion and I felt pretty good just driving like this, just the two of us.

But right after the intersection of 37 and 115, I noticed that the billboard that had advertised La-Z-Boy recliners for years had been pasted over completely white and someone had already climbed up, probably last night, and painted, in sloppy black letters, Fish and Whiskey. Just that. No directions, no address, just Fish and Whiskey, and I knew that was the kind of place my father would take me, some backwoods dive, a jukebox blasting and some middle-aged waitress with stiff blonde hair yelling in orders for deep fry across the bar. Even one drink there would make me sick. And as quick as that, I wanted out of the station wagon, out of this evening. I wanted to say, "Turn around" or "Get out of here before you ruin everything, before you poison the only chance I've got." It was a mistake to have thought he'd fit, even for the time it took for dinner, in a designer home among people who loved and trusted the arts. I might even have turned to say that to him, but he spoke first and he spoke quietly, gently, and without reproach. He said, "I've earned this loneliness. Right now you don't think you want it, and maybe you don't, but it exists, and if you do return someday, you'll honor this inheritance. You'll understand it then."

"I hate this place," I said, and he said back, "Sometimes so do I."

"Then why have you stayed so long with nothing?"

"Lives are not interchangeable," he said. "Jackie Robinson for Pope Paul. Henry Ford for the Hunchback of Notre Dame. You don't simply reject the character of place and genes, contesting your whole life as though the choice existed to accept another, a better one, without coming to grief."

"Better ones do exist," I argued, half-shouting now. "Much better ones."

"You mean the Crouch sanctuary? That fiction?"

"It's real," I said. "It's real to me, so let's just drop it— this whole conversation."

My father nodded. "Okay," he said, and I don't know why I turned on him the way I did. But I said (and I was staring right at him), "If this is the life you want, fine, but don't ruin mine too!"

"Too?" my father said, slowing the car.

"That's right. Too, also, as well as. What I'm saying is, don't force your suffer-more-expect-less philosophy on me. Don't blab that line anymore. It's garbage. It plain stinks."

I knew, when he pulled off sharply onto the road's dry shoulder, that he wasn't going to drag out the argument or turn on me close up, guilt style, and ask how could I speak to my own father like that, how? That wasn't his way. He pulled over so I could drive the last few miles to the Crouches' house, since I seemed so sure of the way—an escape route, as I'd come to believe, from my father's miserable world that refused to yield, pursuing and pursuing, not wanting me ever to get away.

I nosed the car into the long driveway and stopped. There was bright sunlight on the plants in the hall windows, and the leaves were very green, corporeal and magnified, and I knew there would be a mist on the inside of the glass, the way there always was on the insides of greenhouses, and when you breathed deeply you'd get a little dizzy, a little high. That's the ecstatic feeling I always had arriving at the Crouches', of things growing whole and pure. And if my father could only sense that, he'd forgive everything I'd said. He'd understand what it was I refused to lose and he'd back off, get behind the steering wheel again and drive right out of there, for now anyway, sensing that he didn't belong.

But he didn't do that. He said, "Turn off the car." I tried, but the motor did that cheap-gas knocking routine, and I switched the key back on. "Maybe that's a hint," my father said, and smiled. Maybe it was, but I put the car in neutral and let up on the brake, and we coasted, as though in slow motion, down the gradual decline and parked by the front door. The motor shut right off this time when I turned the key, and my father, with his first joke in a long time, asked, "Should we lock it up?" and I said, "Come on—let's go," now that we'd finally settled on going in.

I didn't need to ring the Crouches' doorbell (I hadn't done that for months—Phoebe had given me a key so I could come and go as I pleased), but I rang it anyhow, I guess for the formality of being properly received. I had asked Phoebe to keep an eye out for us, but it was Bissell who answered. He said to my father, "What's your first name?"

"Andy," my father said, and Bissell started in singing Shirley Ellis's "The Name Game":

> *"Andy Andy bo bandy banana fana fo fandy,*
> *me mi mo nandy, Andy."*

He went through a couple of verses, spastic and laughing. He hated spoilsports, people who tried distracting him from being his usual jerky self. His mother was the worst offender, carrying on about the importance of first impressions and how a bad one could start rumors floating, possibly staining your reputation later on in life. Bissell said he didn't care one iota about later on in life, and Mr. Crouch usually backed him. He'd say, "Me either." He'd say, "Survivors always remain immune to threats in the future." Phoebe's refrain was always, "Like father, like son."

I stayed out of it completely, saying nothing, but I admired that male Crouch refusal to be tamed and thought how different that seemed from what my father usually bad-mouthed about the rich—their willingness to sell out to any profit or scandal. But right now I figured my father, standing in the doorway being serenaded, was probably thinking, and with good reason, Who is this loony, so I said, trying to distract Bissell, "What's for dinner?" and he started in again:

> "Chink Chink bo bink banana fana fo fink,
>   me mi mo mink, Chink."

And he did a lot of ah, so's, bowing and bowing as he led us toward the delectable smells of fried rice and wonton soup and pu pu platters, down the hallway, as long and wide as a street, I thought, a back street in exotic Hong Kong, no place a local like my father had ever been.

Nor had I, but the Crouches had talked often about someday sending me and Phoebe to visit cities on their *should see* list: Pittsburgh to digest the genius of Frank Lloyd Wright, San Francisco for shopping at Fisherman's Wharf, New York City for a day at the Met, dinner that night at The Russian Tea Room. I was always excited, expectant, but Phoebe acted only lukewarm about any excursions, having been bored by Europe half a dozen times. So we left travel on the back burner, but I was making inroads anyway, memorizing names and touring America at night before falling asleep. I wondered if the Crouches had in mind to rent us a room together, a double bed, and I visualized over and over what that would be like, every detail, right down to the scalloped gold nozzles of the bathtub, the splinters of moonlight glinting on the inside of Phoebe's thigh. And no matter how infinite the possibilities, the world always seemed a manageable size. I had an explorer's eye (years ago one of my teachers had even told me that), so I just couldn't buy into my father's small town theory about place and genes, how we should stay where we belonged.

Not that he was completely blind to the world, but things got real blurry for him a long time back. I'd never pinpointed it exactly, but I guess it really started the morning my mother died and got worse and worse until he finally lost the farm and the two of us moved into town. He stared a lot in those days, usually at nothing, at least nothing anybody else could ever make out. Even so, he was always a man with certain insights, usually about how people were treated decently or not. And with a rifle or bow he had the best aim of anyone I had ever seen, and he spotted everything—the slightest movement in the woods or a single droplet of mud on a leaf where a deer had stepped out of the swamp. It could be I inherited that. I hope so.

But he had tunnel vision too, and that's what got him in fights and almost landed him in the slammer a bunch of times. That was my father at his worst, flaunting that narrow focus, redneck style, wanting instead to flatten things, people and art and ideas, requiring they be simple and dimensionless, something he could appraise straight up—no nonsense, quickly, and at face value.

So I wasn't buying into his campaign about the allegiance of sons to their fathers, his speculation about replacement and how I should (even worse, was obligated) to carry on the family name, its traditions and values. Nope, not this kid, not without a lot of modifications and the reassurance that I could decide for myself in the end what was worth salvaging or not. It was possible I'd regret this attitude someday. My father said he was sure I would and that it would return to haunt me. He said the history of even one small life should not vanish so fast, and though it irked me to hear him say that, I knew, deep down, it was the part of him that I loved most.

Bissell led us into the living room, the tips of his fingers pressed together under his chin (all he needed was a long, thin beard), and then, nodding in the direction of his father, who sat alone, he said, "Ah, so, one Crouch on one couch," as though he were providing the text of an ancient Chinese painting. I half expected to see Mr. Crouch, eyes closed, meditating under a straw hat.

The Crouches were big on ethnic dining, and a few months back Mrs. Crouch had served an entire week of her Chef's Choice World Sampler—kulebiaka from Russia one night; Latvian straw potatoes the next; from Greece, moussaka; from Spain, paella, my favorite. The meals were authenticated by the appropriate drink, ouzo or chilled vodka or sangria on ice, whatever was called for. The Crouches had every kind of booze imaginable stockpiled in their liquor closet—even bottles of tequila with a fat white worm in each, bloated worms that Phoebe explained were there on purpose, but she couldn't remember what the purpose was.

Bissell liked to shake those bottles to see if the worms were still alive. He said, "I wouldn't swallow one sip of that for a million bucks. N capital O. No way!" I thought maybe that stuff was just for show, but the night we did eat Mexican I was nervous Mr. Crouch might break out a bottle, 180 proof. I didn't want to have to say, "No, thanks"—I'd promised myself to try everything offered by this new life, even what puzzled or frightened me at first. If I had no taste for a particular food or drink, I'd have to acquire one, unlike my father, who couldn't stomach foreign cuisine or fancy liqueurs of any kind. Give him a cold Stroh's or a boilermaker any day—a man's drink. He said once he'd retch on the diet of the rich. I wondered if he meant tequila worms, but I figured not. I was sure he had never heard of such a thing.

Sometimes Mr. Crouch stacked records on the stereo, talk records (though Bissell and Phoebe hated these) describing the particular country whose food we were eating, its culture and politics, a kind of audio travelogue. But mostly he'd just select music to set the mood—Ravi Shankar for Indian night, shakuhachi for Japanese. Nobody ever dressed in costume, and I was relieved it was no different on this night of my father's first and probably final visit.

What I knew for sure was that the huge world atlas would be open to China, and whoever was interested after dinner, Mr. Crouch would take on a tour through a configuration of cities and mountain ranges and waterways. Mrs. Crouch was always mesmerized by her husband's vast knowledge of people and places, and in comparison, she understood the irrelevance of the rest of mankind, those toilers who made up the enormous populations of continents, but whom she could imagine only as servants, the ones who cleaned the houses of the wealthy in Michigan's suburbs. "I've never had a maid," she'd say every now and then, as though this fact had just dawned on her for the first time.

"That's okay," Mr. Crouch would respond. "That's okay. If we wanted one, we could certainly afford it."

I was right: the atlas was wide open on the cushion beside Mr. Crouch, but that's not what he was reading. He was reading through his *Circumpolar Vortex*, the title he'd given to a brown ledger where he recorded ideas for inventions, brainstorms of unusual shifts and proportion. He said his best ones had never caught on. But he did own one patent for which royalties still trickled in. This was his Wheelchair

Mop, a dry mop for collecting dust and spiderwebs spun in the corners of ceilings. It was ultralightweight, and the tubular aluminum extension handle allowed even a grandmother seventy-five, eighty years old who still believed it mattered to spiff up the house or apartment, with a sitting reach of nine feet. They sold like hotcakes at first, especially throughout the new senior citizen high rises in Detroit and Chicago and Buffalo, cities where the product took hold, mostly through word of mouth. Mr. Crouch said who knew, really, how big it might have gone with the right promo, an aggressive advertising pitch? My father had fancied himself an inventor of sorts too, years ago, and he said that to Mr. Crouch after I introduced them and they shook hands. Then they started swapping invention ideas—Mr. Crouch's clear glass bathtub for my father's reversible shoes, Mr. Crouch's hard rubber tombstones for my father's tree bark camouflage. They went on like that for half an hour until Phoebe, stepping from the kitchen and ringing a tiny bell, announced, "Dinnertime." I could see Mr. Crouch wanted to stay right there talking. He was having a blast.

"Before we eat," he said to my father, "tell me your single wildest invention brainstorm, your wildest, best ever."

I don't think my father was being a smart aleck when he answered, but it sure was a strange thing to say, nothing I'd ever heard from him. He said, "A machine that would crush words like 'ambience' and 'milieu' and 'ennui.' "

"How come?" Bissell the word lover asked, confused. But Mr. Crouch agreed with my father without explanation. He said, "I know what you mean. Something to blow them to kingdom come!"

The rest of the evening continued like that, tense sometimes and always a little strange, but friendly too. The only time I thought my father might be ticked was when Mrs. Crouch, appearing for the first time, asked, "Hands washed, everyone?" My father held his up, palms facing out. They were badly stained from having handled thousands and thousands of tires at the Fisk. "You need Boraxo," she said. "There's a can by the washbasin in the garage. And a scrub brush." My father just smiled, said, "Pleased to meet you," and sat down at the table. For a few seconds the rest of us stood behind our chairs. My father said, "Smells great," and he lifted his glass of sake and downed it in one long gulp. I knew he couldn't stand the taste, but he didn't let on. He even asked for a refill, not a quick hitter this time, but something to sip throughout the meal, which he said several times was the best Chinese food he'd ever had, better even than Danny Ho Ho's. I believed him, the way he ate, pushing aside the chopsticks in favor of a teaspoon that was sitting out on a saucer like something nobody else intended to use.

There was no ashtray, so my father flicked his Pall Mall on the edge of his plate. He said when he was a kid his favorite part of eating oriental was the fortune cookie at the end. I knew there would be some—the Crouches didn't miss a trick. What I didn't know was that Bissell had typed the fortunes, and without getting to read even one, Mrs. Crouch had folded the soft dough carefully around them and placed them on a cookie sheet, which she slid into the oven. They were perfect now, brittle wedges, and when his mother brought them out in a white bowl, Bissell, who had settled into quiet repose, jumped up shouting, "I'll do it. I want to pass them out." And since he had the floor, while he was the center of attention again for a change, he wanted to recommend a book, by title and author, that we all should read. "It's Chinese."

Mrs. Crouch, beaming, said, "Oh, good for you, Bissell," but I could tell he was about to crack up over a joke he'd been saving all day. The book, he said, was called *The Ruptured Duck*, by One Hung Low.

Phoebe said, "Pathetic," while Bissell spun in circles into the drapes. He was hoarse by the time he'd finished laughing and sat back down and said about the fortune cookies, "Right around the table. You're first, Phoebe. You have to read it out loud."

Phoebe did not snap her fortune cookie in the middle. She bit off the very end and slid out the thin white tongue of paper. She read while Bissell made a big show of covering his ears, as though what we were about to hear was too much. The fortune was written in OP talk, the letters O and P following every consonant:

"GOP-OO-DOP SOP-E-XOP
COP-O-MOP-I-NOP-GOP."

Translated, it said, "Good sex coming." I was glad Mrs. Crouch hadn't picked that one. Had she, I'm sure I would have blushed. I just couldn't imagine her kicking off her Pappagallos and hiking up her dress for some action in the hammock on the back deck or on the thick carpet of the hall, or anywhere else, for that matter. She was the most sexless woman I'd ever seen. It puzzled me how she'd had these two children. Especially her only daughter, who, on our very first date, had taken me so naturally to bed.

I read my fortune next:

"Soon the dark river.
Two crows, two blackbirds."

Phoebe said, "That's weird, Bissell," but I kind of liked it. It reminded me of a haiku, though it did seem too bleak a sign, no moon shining.

"All set?" It was my father talking. He had taken his reading glasses from his shirt pocket and put them on, but he still held his fortune a long way from his face. "Can't quite make it out," he said, and Bissell hustled around from the other side of the table.

"I'll do it," he said. "I'll read it for you.

> " 'Two paths diverged in a woods.'
> You've taken the wrong one. Un*fortun*ately
> it's too late to go back.

"That's my antifortune," Bissell said, and Mrs. Crouch, recognizing the Robert Frost line (she'd been a lit major at Smith), said, "Good for you, Bissell."

"That's the one I worked hardest on," he said.

"I can tell," said Mrs. Crouch, "and I'm glad our guest was the one to pick it. It's an important message, to push on even in the wrong direction." And that's what my father announced we had to be doing, pushing on once the last three fortunes were read. I had to get up early to scumbust, and I guess my father had in mind to spend a little time alone, maybe watching the late movie on TV. Bissell said we all got to keep our own fortunes, but when he left the room Mrs. Crouch asked my father for his back. "I hope you don't mind," she said. "I like to write down all the smart things my children say." My father had already rolled up his fortune to the size of a spitball. When Mrs. Crouch opened her hand, he dropped it into the tiny well in the center of her palm. There was hardly anything left but smudgy pulp.

Just enough, I thought, to flick from his thumbnail on the way out.

I told Phoebe I wasn't going to use the MGB. I'd ride home with my father and drive the station wagon to work. That felt like the right way to finish the night, though I felt hungry for a few minutes alone with Phoebe in the observatory, a slow dance or two under a heaven of stars. Mr. Crouch patted my father on the back and invited him over anytime for more invention talk, but I knew he'd never come, never. I also knew that by morning Mr. Crouch wouldn't remember my father ever having been there. Perhaps he'd have some vague recollection of some reversible shoes or tree bark camouflage. But all that would be suffused, muted in the larger context of more significant realities—the business of blueprints, for example, the steady work for which he was extravagantly paid.

Bissell was the last one to leave us. He walked us outside to the car and said to me, "Hold on to your tongue and say, 'I gave my teacher an apple.' " I tried, and it came out, all the words a little slurred, "I gave my teacher an asshole."

"Did you hear it? Did you hear what you said?" He was choking so bad from laughing that I had to smack him pretty hard between the shoulder blades to get it stopped. After a minute, as soon as he was okay again, he said to my father, "You try it too," and my father said, "You try this one instead: 'My daddy owns a shipyard.' " Bissell stuck out his tongue and grabbed hold and started in: "My daddy owns a shityard, my daddy owns a shityard." This, Bissell would never forget. He'd remember my father as a friend forever.

It was bright out, moon bright, and I watched through the

windshield for two shooting stars to intersect. Phoebe said that was the ultimate moment of love, that millisecond it took them to pass. My father had the radio on, and Ferlin Husky was singing one of my favorites, "On the Wings of a Dove." I thought, So many things in flight, the spirit included, and the mind in its constant orbit of uncertainty. Sometimes it made a guy go crazy, all that space and motion, but other times it would almost rock him into perfect sleep. I was hoping my father wouldn't talk, that he'd feel the peacefulness too and maybe stop on the 31 bridge for a few minutes so we could watch whatever light was floating by on the river. He pulled in instead at the Crystal Bar.

"I could sure use a cold beer after all that sake and soy sauce," he said, and crossing the parking lot, he flipped me a quarter for the jukebox. "We won't stay but ten, fifteen minutes." The place was clean, like in the Hemingway short story we read for English class earlier in the year, and I understood for the first time why it was the old man in that story drank where he did every night, in "a clean, well-lighted place." My father straddled a bar stool and ordered two Stroh's. I punched the buttons, 4-R, for that same Ferlin Husky song, and my father spun slowly around and said smiling, "We just heard that one for free." Then the song came up a second time and then a third. There were only two other guys sitting at the far end of the bar, and the bigger of them, looking right at us in the dark diagonal of the mirror, asked, "Ain't but one song in that quarter?"

My father took a long, slow sip of beer and then sucked the foam away from his upper lip. "Looks to me," he said, "like the boy's the one paying." He didn't sound mean, and hearing it like that, the two of them nodded and turned away.

The bartender folded his white towel over the spigot and drew himself just half a draft. "Slow night," he said, and my father, throwing his arm around my shoulder, said, "You know what I think?" and he paused and then he said, "I think it's a damn good thing we came."

F O U R

I skipped school the day Phoebe left for Smith College. I'd seen her the night before, and we'd been over everything—letters and phone call times and vacation dates I already knew by heart. I wanted to see Phoebe off, maybe just stand at the head of the driveway and wave good-bye, but Mrs. Crouch thought it best that I didn't drop over while they were trying to organize and pack the car and get started east. I felt pretty bad being left out like that, but Phoebe explained that it was going to be real crazy over there and that her mother got all nervous before trips. The whole family was driving out in the Lincoln Continental. The MGB stayed. Smith College didn't allow freshmen to bring cars, so Phoebe gave it to me to use for the year while she was away.

The last drive we took together that September was to the Hillside Esso, where Phoebe filled the tank with premium on the Crouch charge. "My Boy Lollipop" was playing on the radio, and the guy pumping gas was mouthing the words, and although he glanced up and raised his eyebrows in acknowledgment, he didn't stop his silent singing when Phoebe said, "Danny, this is my boyfriend, and he has permission to charge here anytime." Danny nodded, still held by the Caribbean blue beat of fifteen-year-old Millie Small, and I was certain he'd never remember me (though he'd seen me in the MGB with Phoebe dozens of times) if I really did have to stop here in a pinch.

I had never charged anything in my life. Phoebe said once, "Oh, don't be so provincial," but my father had always lectured me against the trap of charging, saying he had no intention of ever being "on the books" to anyone or of owning a credit card for gas or clothes or anything else, period, done. He said if you couldn't pay cash up front for it, you shouldn't be buying it in the first place, whatever it was.

"Check the oil?" Danny asked, and Phoebe said, "It's fine," and Danny handed her a sales pad, which she signed "Phoebe C." As he was folding those small pages over and tearing out the yellow receipt, he started singing again, but this time loud enough for me to hear:

> "My boy Lollipop,
> You made my heart go giddy-up,
> You're as sweet as candy,
> You're my Sugar Dandy. . . ."

Danny handed the receipt to Phoebe, who handed it to me, and I shoved it in among the others in the glove compartment. Phoebe said, "See ya, Danny," and Danny, not knowing or caring that she'd be gone for three solid months, said, "Right-o." I remember that clearly, the "Right-o," and the way the bell sounded from inside the station (a double ring for each set of tires) when we drove over the black hose by the pumps, and how "My Boy Lollipop" stayed in my head for days.

I was humming it when Phoebe phoned to say they were finally off to Massachusetts. "We're on our way out the door," she said. It was almost noon. Usually the receiver would be off the hook while my father, who was working nights, napped, so I was right there to answer the phone on the first half ring. We talked only a few minutes, but before Phoebe hung up she said, "Go up to the observatory tonight. I left a present there for you." Until she said that, I had been pretty disappointed by our conversation, one I had waited for for over three hours. At such a crucial time, our words seemed oddly ordinary, attenuated, as if some filmy membrane were blocking the natural flow of feelings from our throats. It wasn't that we were choked up—it wasn't that at all. Phoebe had cried a lot the night before, and we had all that out of our systems. I guess we simply had nothing left to say, a blank postscript, the vacant feeling always accompanying such long departures.

Funny how the MGB felt so much like mine on the drive over to the Crouches'. I knew my father wouldn't like me having it, gas included—not this way, without having worked to meet a single payment. And I knew he'd make a stink about not boxing him in in the driveway so that he'd have to jockey cars, and how the garage was for the station wagon and the station wagon only. But I didn't care. What I knew was that it felt good just to be driving at night with the top down and WKBW playing tunes all the way from Buffalo, four or five without interruption.

Phoebe and her parents trusted me with the car, and I'd take immaculate care of it—no two ways about that. I'd wash it in the backyard every weekend with the hose and soapy bucket and sponge, the way my father always did with his cars, keeping them looking good even when they were old. But unlike him I'd drive then to someplace secluded, some-place over on Lake Michigan, the leaves just turning, and

I'd open a new container of Meguiar's Mirror Glaze and bear down, waxing in hard, deep circles until, chamoised clean, that cirrus white finish would shimmer, brilliant in the fall sun. And I'd keep the MGB tuned and I wouldn't get carried away downshifting a lot, double clutching and redlining the tac before shifting gears, the way Phoebe liked me to on the curvy back roads, especially those newly blacktopped. I was a good driver (even Mr. Crouch said that), and with Phoebe next to me I was never scared when we'd hit top end on the long straightaway before heading home. There would be none of that now though, no matter what songs were tempting my weakest impulse to steal the night. No "Dead Man's Curve" or "Tell Laura I Love Her." No, sir, no tragedy for this kid. I'd take it slow for a while, putting only what miles I really needed on the car, essential miles, like the ones I'd travel that night to pick up my present.

I'd never seen the Crouch house so dark and I felt kind of funny sitting there in Phoebe's car in the driveway. It wasn't like Mr. Crouch to want to save on electricity, so I figured the automatic timer must have given up the ghost. Normally there were floods on everywhere, spraying light from beneath the rhododendrons. Maybe I should have turned on a couple of lamps inside or at least turned on the porch light, but I had already decided to stay all night in the observatory, and I'd simply have to get up and patrol a few times against intruders. After all, it was my duty, as someone who half lived there, to protect those grounds, and one thing for sure was that I wouldn't back off from any attack—I wouldn't give up one morsel of the enormous surplus of riches stockpiled by the Crouches. I even thought for a minute about driving back home for a shotgun or deer rifle, but I suppressed that crazy instinct—inherited, I suppose, from my father, who always kept one loaded, first at the farm and now in the apartment, the gun to go for, he told me over and over while I was growing up, if ever I heard any strange noises, something or someone approaching I knew should not be there.

But there was no reason to be armed at the Crouches'. It was quiet all night, and all I heard for the hours I stayed awake were the 45s Phoebe had stacked on the stereo in the observatory. She'd left me a note in a pink, perfumed envelope, explaining that the songs were arranged in a certain order and that I should lie down on the cot and listen to them (each had its own message) before opening my present. It will mean more that way, the note said.

They were our favorites, almost all slow ones, and I closed my eyes and imagined us dancing cheek to cheek as we did some nights, the observatory transformed by moonlight into a ballroom. It was cooler now, but during the summer months Phoebe would always be barefoot. And sometimes, if it was too hot, she'd stop dancing right in the middle of a song and arch her back a little and raise both arms straight up so I could lift her T-shirt over her head. She was always braless, and when she'd press up hard against me, I'd undo the button of her shorts, not to take them off, but for the feeling that so much had happened with just a twist of the thumb and finger—that little V of cloth hanging open, the zipper still up. I knew she'd pull it down later on and step out of those shorts. It was almost automatic when she heard certain songs, like the Shirelles' "Will You Still Love Me Tomorrow?" And that's the record that dropped onto the turntable first, and I understood at that moment how naturally we followed each other's leads, together beneath millions of stars, and how we would never know loss or separation, the subject of all those slow songs we played so often, feeling good in the harmony of that loneliness, as long as we had each other to hold.

I listened to "I Will Follow Him" and "Come Softly to Me," the whole time holding on to the present. I decided to open it when Ivory Joe Hunter started singing:

> *"Since I met you Baby,*
> *My whole life has changed.*
> *Since I met you Baby,*
> *My whole life has changed.*
> *And everybody tells me*
> *That I'm not the same."*

Phoebe had used thin white wrapping paper, like Kleenex, and she must have kept folding it over and over, pressing it between her lips, because there were perfect, red O's of lipstick covering it. She was creative that way, always designing things and tie-dyeing expensive material for dresses, or hand painting greeting cards with watercolors, muted purples and greens and yellows. She once even cut a large potato in half, and on each of the two flat ends, as though they were linoleum blocks, she carved a single image, the astronomical sign of the moon. Then she re-inked her father's stamp pads, a black and a red, and with only those two colors she pressed the image hundreds of times at different angles on what looked like a roll of blank white wallpaper. I thought maybe Mrs. Crouch would hire someone to cover a wall with it. It was that nice. When I said to Phoebe, "I bet that process has never been done before," she said back, "Yep, it has. Henri Matisse, right before he died." And then she speculated about the price of a Matisse original, what just one potato print would bring at auction in New York.

But I didn't really care if Phoebe ever sold anything she made—it simply didn't matter to me. What I knew was that no art could be more valuable to me than the image of Phoebe's full lips on the gift wrapping. Nothing could be more original than that—no still life of roses, no reclining nude. I had kissed those lips for real. I had seen her lick them under the skylight where sometimes she'd stand naked gazing up, and maybe they'd part just a little and I'd see the white edge of her teeth, her tongue like a shadow, and these, the details perfected, would hold me spellbound for as long as she stayed there posing, re-creating the sensuous landscape of herself.

Had Phoebe been with me in the observatory, she would have said, "Just rip the paper off—it's no big deal." She was like that with everything she made, willing to destroy it as soon as she was done with it, then move on to another project. I guess that was healthy in some ways, her always rushing to meet new things. But I knew she'd have to do an about-face at Smith, where she had already declared herself a visual arts major. She'd have to build a permanent portfolio, in order to justify the next four years, and take lots of slides, an inventory of her large canvases and sculptures and figure drawings, her ceramic pieces thrown on the wheel. "Borrring," she'd say whenever I launched into that. All she wanted to try (not study—that took all the fun out of it, she said) was glassblowing, something she'd never done, a course not even offered at Smith. She said she'd have to go someplace like Rhode Island School of Design or Kansas City Art Institute, someplace real artsy-fartsy. But what she objected to was how serious the students would be there, all hotshots, she said, and weird too, glimpsing the universe in everything they touched, clamoring all the time for what was immortal in "the work." She had said that real sarcastically, "the work," and she insisted those places were all too ingrown anyway. She'd decided long ago to coast toward whatever it was she was *meant* to become.

I didn't say so, but I could never swallow that "meant to become" stuff. It sounded too much like my father, though for different reasons. I liked much better the idea of acquiring vision that saw beyond the myopic and predictable stare of destiny. Mine had looked pretty bleak for a while, but ever since meeting the Crouches, no future seemed unapproachable anymore, and that future included Phoebe (I'd accept that much on blind faith), who had modeled naked only for me so many nights, not so I could draw or photograph her, but rather so I could learn to love the anatomy of a woman's body anew each time before taking her to bed. She had taught me not to be an idle gazer, a leg or breast man, as some of the guys at school referred to themselves. That was an easy lesson since Phoebe was the only one I wanted to touch, the woman whose lips had kissed the delicate paper I was holding.

I would never crumple it up or save it to reuse the way my father always did with bows and Christmas wrapping. I'd frame it for my bedroom wall and hang it right above my pillow the way some people (usually older people) did a crucifix. I'd title it *Lip Angels* or something like that, something romantic and spiritual too.

And I wouldn't tell Phoebe about having saved it, not until after we'd been married for years. Maybe I'd pull it out on our twenty-fifth wedding anniversary, and we'd return to the observatory (I always assumed we'd inherit the Crouch house and property) under a radiant cluster of stars and replay this whole night, except this time with the two of us together.

I knew I'd remember this night forever. I could feel it

powerfully in my aloneness, knowing Phoebe, at that very moment, was drifting farther and farther east, but leaving me, as a point of reference, this present in a small green plastic case. I attached that much significance to it, as though it were an axis, the exact locus of departure and return, the gravity center by which we retained our balance and leverage through the infinite space of the world.

I opened the case. Inside was Phoebe's diaphragm. She had always inserted it in private, and I had only seen it once before, a strange circle of skin grafted to her palm by the moonlight.

"Touch," she'd said. "It's what protects us." And in an even bigger way than pregnancy, it did, squelching whatever fears I might have had about her meeting someone else. There was no need to worry. First the MGB and now her diaphragm, entrusted to me for safekeeping. Some guys would say they went together, a good car and a good lay, and they'd work the cruddy jobs after school (forget the homework) and summer after summer, saving for the dream of cruising the main streets, hoping for that one magic night at the drive-in movies when Suzie or Jean or Alice Somebody-or-Other would not stop them from going all the way. That was the promise for them of growing up small-town, the universe reduced to the cramped backseat of a 1955 Ford or Chevy. But I was flying high, transported beyond the tiny enclosures of circumstance, that "Whatever happens happens" mentality, and with whomever or wherever. I was sold on Phoebe and Phoebe only. And I was convinced that the combination of college and travel and what I still had to learn about taste and culture and business from the Crouches would determine the extent to which I'd escape the flaccid existence surrounding me here. Maybe it was a little snobby to assume I'd so easily outdistance the local group of hangers-on, but I had a steady girlfriend a year older than me who'd graduated from a private day school and was going to attend Smith College in Massachusetts, and at this very instant I was standing below a huge domed skylight in a very expensive observatory, not checking the sky calendar for a predawn meteor shower, but holding instead Phoebe's diaphragm without embarrassment.

Phoebe always talked about the immaturity of other guys she'd known, guys she'd gone out with. What she liked best about me, she'd often say, was that I was going places, but that unlike the aggressive and pushy career types, I was like soft light, meaning I was easy to be around. And she promised me a bunch of times that I was the one she would always return to. And that's exactly what she was saying again with the gift of the diaphragm. Maybe I couldn't display it like an I.D. bracelet or a ring squeezed onto my little finger, but I could care less. That stuff was a lot of crapola, invented for the showy and childish ceremony of breaking up, of giving things back. No, thanks. I'd stay with the secret of what I had. I'd hide the diaphragm in a drawer at home, beneath my socks and underwear, and I'd take it out the first night Phoebe returned from college, not until.

I felt happy dozing off on the cot in my sleeping bag, but later that night I drifted into a strange dream. In it I had packed a suitcase that I tied to the luggage rack on the trunk of the MGB. The top was up, heater on full blast, and I had decided to drive east, drive all night and surprise Phoebe in her dorm room. I kept losing my bearings. I kept returning, the needle on empty, to Hillside Esso. But it was not Danny who lowered his face next to mine. It was my father bending down with his hands full of maps, road maps of Michigan's

Upper Peninsula, and topographical maps marking the two-tracks into the backwoods, and from there, in markings like thin red veins, footpaths to certain hunting blinds on the edges of dumps and swamps. I could tell he wanted to go with me, though he was silent, his lips moving as Danny's had mouthing lyrics, and I'd throw those wilderness maps out by the pumps, but that's where I'd be headed every time, north again toward the Straits of Mackinac, toward bear country, deer country, where the radio salvaged only a word or two from the static, and then nothing.

And here comes the weirdest part. On those dark roads I'd see my father in his undershirt, though it was very cold out, and he'd be hunched over smoking a cigarette, and he'd turn into the wind to try and wave me down on the outskirts of every dying town. I'd hit the high beams, and he'd cover his eyes, and I'd blow right by him, gas pedal pressed to the floor. After a few miles I'd turn around, crying, but I'd never see him, even though I'd open the car window and stop across the road from where I was sure he'd been standing, shading his eyes against the blindness of the lights, making sure it was me who was passing, leaving him behind again, but heading, at least, in the direction he'd always taken me as a kid, threatening we'd go deeper and deeper next time into the woods, threatening someday we'd stay up there for good.

I awakened, and it was barely daybreak, and I could see what looked like snow clouds through the skylight. September snow clouds, a sure sign of an arctic winter. I was glad not to be at home, my father just returning exhausted and smelling of rubber from his eight hours at the Fisk. I did not want to hear him in the kitchen or have to wait for him to get out of the bathroom so I could get ready for school. I was thankful to wake alone in the known landscape of the observatory,

Phoebe's diaphragm on the table beside me. I didn't understand much about dream analysis, but I figured this one was about trying to break free and getting no place. That's how Phoebe would have interpreted it, but that would never happen to me in real life, all that confusion driving the back roads of regret and indecision, leaving and not leaving, fighting my father's implacable need to keep me from getting lost or hurt.

He might have been opening my bedroom door to wake me right then, not even aware that I was at the Crouches', assuming I'd still be counting z's, getting in a few extra minutes before we'd exchange places. Not literally, but he'd be off to bed, and me, I'd be shaking the cobwebs out as though I'd been driving all night, pushing straight through, a fugitive of sorts, stunned by the first sharp light of the sun in my attempt to get away.

F I V E

And that's what I thought about all first semester—getting away, driving and daydreaming and trying to reignite the fire that had gone right out of my life. Most evenings, just to get out of the house, I'd drive thirty miles to the bluffs overlooking Lake Michigan, and I'd nose the MGB tight to the guardrail and close my eyes and take long, deep breaths. I'd think, What a sham, killing time like this, depressed and lonesome as hell and bored completely out of my skull, the waves breaking a hundred feet below me along the edge of the dunes.

But I couldn't help it—nothing worked, and there was no disguise for my moodiness. My one friend, Mark Elkhart, just a few weeks after Phoebe left for Massachusetts, told me I'd turned into a first-class douche bag, a douche bag *and* a dilettante. "Amherst College this, Smith College that," he said. "What for anyway, huh? What's the point when you've got a full ride at U of M?" Then he said, "You're loony sometimes, you know that?"

We'd been cruising, Mark slouched down in the bucket seat, and with a peashooter, he kept trying to hit the metal road signs as we passed them at fifty, sixty miles per hour.

He'd been on me to room with him. As he'd said, "Let's team up, you and me, and break us some hearts."

Mark had good grades (not like mine, but good) and a family with a lot of money, so I figured he could name his college, write his own ticket, which, he said, meant Ann Arbor, following in his father's footsteps. Mark said he had it sussed—four years in premed, then four more after that, then two interning at Henry Ford Hospital in Detroit—a decade neatly ordered before heading back north to share in his father's practice. Dr. Elkhart, Dr. Elkhart, podiatry. Big bucks, but a lack of vision there.

I had read an article by an Italian scientist who claimed that the Leaning Tower of Pisa was about to fall. I wanted to see it before it did. I wanted to stand next to Phoebe at the opening of a Chagall exhibit. I wanted more surprise in my life, more romance, more expensive wine. I wanted out of Michigan and I said that to Mark, and he said back, "Buddy, get real." He said, "If you care about building a future, then draw up some floor plans that make sense. You're out of your league in Rome or Paris. Wise up, will you? You're out of your league out of state."

Which is all I'd been hearing, from Mark and from my father and from the counselors at school—*Stay here stay here stay here stay here*, a chorus of nay sayers, the stay-at-homers, every one of them singing off-key, out of pitch. All scratchy notes, I thought, the din of those ugly voices pounding in my head, songs I imagined with titles like "Let Me Clue You In," or "Listen Up," or "You're Living a Pipe Dream."

"Dime store advice," I told him. "Mark," I said, "you have a slumlord mentality," and, looking right at me, he said back, "You're the one lives in a rat shack, Buddy, not me. Where do you get off with this Mr. Aficionado stuff anyway, like the rest of us are all lowlifes for defending the home front."

For a few seconds I wanted to stop the car and turn off the motor and punch him as hard as I could in the face. Instead, I just slowed down and swung a U-turn and said to him, "Let's call it a night."

"Call it whatever you want," he said. "What the hell," and he turned away from me then and stared out the window, stared without saying another word. I turned on the radio and, a half hour later, when I pulled up in front of his house, I was tapping my fingers on the steering wheel, keeping time to the Beach Boys. Mark opened the car door and got out, but before shutting it he said, "I didn't mean what I said about you living in a rat shack, Buddy. I didn't mean that, no kidding, I didn't." He paused and then he said, "I'm sorry," and when he did I cranked up the volume and shifted into first and, when he shut the door, I squealed the tires in all four gears, trying to get as far away from him as fast as I could.

The very next day (I remember it was a Saturday) I received a letter from the Amherst College admissions office—I'd been accepted, early decision. And it was weird, but I felt both happy and not happy, frightened even. The letter said how they'd loved my personal essay, where I mentioned how I was saving real hard for college and reading Keats and that my mother had died suddenly when I was just a little kid and that I liked Dorothea Lange's Great Depression photographs. I had mentioned also how some northern Michigan faces, my father's included, reminded me a lot of her subjects, staring unguardedly back at the world, almost dreaming. And finally, I said that my father worked a crazy, crazy schedule, taking as much overtime as he could get each week. I used words like "frailty" and "breakable" to describe the tenuous balance of any life assailed by loss or debt, how a busted water pipe or a single car repair could break the spirit of a family for good. And it was worse farther north, the silence, I mean, the way nobody would ever answer you, not even with a nod, as though, at dusk on their front porches, they kept posing over and over for the same expressionless portrait. I made it obvious in the essay that I wanted desperately to be long gone from here and not, quoting Keats for emphasis, *"live in this world alone but in a thousand worlds."* Maybe that part was a little heavy-handed, unfair even, but I figured it was also the voice of passion, the voice of amplitude, and anyway, I was sure that nobody from this neck of the woods, nobody I knew anyhow, had a single urge to edit anything I'd said.

As Mark had said to me once, "We'll watch you fail on your own." And maybe he was right, and if he was, beating out guys from the hotshot private academies like Exeter and Deerfield and Mt. Hermon would be no consolation. At best it would make for flimsy conversation years later: "Such and such a place admitted me, recruited me hard, but I couldn't go, money mostly. I didn't have the bucks." Who cared? Already it sounded like failure, a simpleminded boast to conceal the commonplace, an in-state education.

Amherst had no financial statement on file for me, no way to appraise my need for a scholarship, and my father had made it perfectly clear months ago that he was not about to make public across half a continent his hourly wage at the Fisk. As far as he was concerned, I was on my way down to Ann Arbor in the fall, to attend the University of Michigan on a full tuition waiver, four years renewable. He said to me, "You can't do better." His buddies at work said to him, "Congratulations. Good for your boy," and they meant it.

I'm only guessing that the essay is what got me in to Amherst—probably it did, that and my SATs—but if I was heading east to college it meant I'd arrive paying full freight, which was more money than my father made in an entire year. Not saved, made! And before taxes!

I phoned Phoebe at her dormitory at Smith that night at our usual time (I reversed the charges as usual, as agreed) and she said, listen, she was sending Amherst a hundred-dollar deposit to hold me a spot. No, she said, it wasn't refundable but to stop worrying, for God's sake, and then she talked on and on about work-study programs and low-interest student loans that didn't have to be paid back for years (her roommate had one, no big deal) and about me moving into an apartment with her on Crenshaw Avenue, one her father had already arranged for beginning June 1, which meant free room and board for me and I'd have the MGB to drive to classes and back each day, just like if we were married.

Then she calmed me down by saying, "Buddy, please. This is what we're after. This is what we want, isn't it? To be together, to live together?"

"Yes," I said.

I said, "I'm just spooked about the money—that's all. I'm nervous and I miss you and I'm going half-nuts alone here, and now you're not even going to be here for Christmas—you're not even coming home."

She had dropped that bomb on me during our last conversation—her parents were taking her and Bissell to the Cayman Islands for the whole vacation. And I, having fabricated months' worth of scenes of the two of us alone in the observatory, would spend the holidays instead with my father. He'd decorate the apartment by taping the few Christmas cards we'd receive to the doorjamb in the living room. And he'd cook a canned ham, which we'd eat, saying almost nothing. I couldn't understand why the Crouches hadn't invited me, but I didn't say that to Phoebe. I only said, "Whoopee," when she carried on about how she'd be out for spring break in less than three months.

"Which will feel like three years," I said.

"That's exactly why you have to get out here," she said. "We can't keep on with this long-distance romance. It'll never work, Buddy." And that's how she ended the conversation, saying, "You just get out here," and I said, "I will, I promise—on June fifteenth, I'll be there," which was two days after my high school graduation. I already knew I was going to be valedictorian and would have to hang around for the ceremony as an example of someone who'd be heard from, "loud and clear," Mr. Devine, the principal, had told me, in the years to come.

S I X

I guess Phoebe's deposit did the trick because I was flooded with invitations to "get acquainted" parties in the Midwest, in places like Shaker Heights and Lake Forest and Winnetka, but nothing in Michigan, and on the map (an inch equaled forty miles) those towns were a full day's drive.

Phoebe, home for spring break finally, the snow almost gone from the ground, said forget all that hubbub and concentrate on what's essential, which first of all was to locate a copy of my father's income tax statement for the past couple of years or some legal documents on the foreclosure of our farm seven years earlier. Or, she said, even a weekly stub from his paycheck if that was the best I could do—anything that would show clearly I qualified heavy duty for financial aid, which, as Phoebe put it, was there for the taking.

"Are you sure?" I asked her, the two of us climbing the dark stairs to the observatory. "It doesn't feel right to me. I don't know."

"I'm sure," she said, and stopped suddenly and turned around before opening the door, and she said, "What's that word you use, Buddy? Copacetic? Well, that's what this is— it's copacetic. What we do, we do, and it *has* to be okay. God," she said, "don't peter out on me now," and when she kissed me on the forehead from the stair above, I put my hands on her waist.

"I'm all right," I said, and when I did, she took both my wrists, lifting slowly until each of my palms was cupping a breast, cupping them under her sweatshirt.

"I want to feel you do this to me every day," she said, and she was holding on to the banister, then rocking just slightly back and forth, her eyes closed, and she said, "I love to be touched like this, Buddy," and I stared beyond her at the hook of a moon and at the millions of stars, and I don't know why, but I was tempted to wave, as though I were saying hello or good-bye. Which is what Phoebe complained we were always doing. And I thought right then, Whatever in this life it takes, whatever it takes. I said that to Phoebe, who started a kind of silent applause, clapping with her fingertips just inches from my face.

"Bravo," she said, and a few minutes later, my fingers spread wide inside the elastic waistband of her panties, we were slow dancing right beneath the skylight, dancing and oblivious to the world beyond the two of us until the record started to skip, "Ev'rybody's, Ev'rybody's, Ev'rybody's," and Phoebe stomped her foot on the floor and the song continued, "somebody's fool," and Phoebe said, "Hey! Guess what, we don't have to use that gizmo anymore," meaning her diaphragm, which I had brought up and placed on the cot. "I'm on the pill," she said, trying to sound casual, but she didn't. It sounded rehearsed, and I felt the sensation of that line being staged, delivered on cue, but instead of responding, I felt myself clenching my jaw, clenching it tighter and tighter, wanting to ask her what for and why she hadn't told me last night when she did use the diaphragm, or made believe she did, taking it from me and going into the bathroom.

But I said none of that. Instead, I leaned my head back and marveled at the configuration of the stars, how they always seemed intact, though moving, and how, conversely, the tiny orbit of our own lives seemed more and more out of whack, the record skipping again, and this time Phoebe pulled away from me, for just a sec, as she put it, to turn the stereo off.

Then she said something strange to me from across the room. She said, and I could tell she was mad, "Buddy, why don't you let me do the banking?" I knew she wasn't talking only about money this time, knew it even better when she pulled her sweatshirt back on over her head and folded her arms and stared at me through the thin, diffused light.

"Meaning?" I asked.

"Meaning you went all tense when I told you I was on the pill. Lots of my friends are. It's not exactly radical."

"Are they sleeping around?"

"What you mean is, am *I* sleeping around? That's what you mean, but I haven't been," and then she started to cry. "Damn you, Buddy," she said, "you shouldn't do this," and she wiped her eyes with the back of her hand. "What I want to happen never does," she said. "You won't let it. You're going to lose me, Buddy—I know it," and she started crying even harder, and that's when I went to her and said, "Shh, shh," and I led her to the double cot, and I noticed that the clock radio said 1:30 A.M. when she lay down, then me on top of her. I watched the orange dial for a long time after that, watched the seconds ticking and listened to the lightness of Phoebe breathing, asleep.

She did not wake when I got up and got dressed and covered her with a quilt. Nor when I tiptoed down the stairs, nor when I started the MGB. Or if she did, no lights came on in the observatory. The note I left her said only that we'd talk for real in the morning. And then the P.S., where I mentioned how I'd seen a comet with two brilliant, luminous green tails burn out right above the skylight. It reminded me of some exotic, heavenly fish, I said, and you, sleeping, remind me of an angel.

Mrs. Crouch served us cantaloupe and toast and marmalade and a pot of coffee. She'd just gotten back from the airport and now she was off again, this time to Justine's to get her hair done, a ritual she maintained every time her husband perished for a day, as she put it, meaning only that he'd flown downstate on business. And Bissell, who was still a week away from vacation, had already boarded the bus to school before I'd arrived.

I wasn't looking at Phoebe—I was standing at the window that cantilevered over the patio, staring at the purple crocuses that had blossomed right through the snow. And at Black Creek in the distance, where Bissell had first ignited one of his homemade bombs for me—he'd said we were on maneuvers; we were blowing the enemy to kingdom come. But it was quiet now, a thin fog lifting and dissipating from the valley. When Phoebe did speak finally, all she said was, "Truce?" and I nodded and then I turned around.

"I want to be with you out east," I said, "I don't care how. You do the banking," I said, and I smiled then and she did too, and she said to me, "Come over here. Buddy, Buddy, Buddy," she said, and when I sat down, the chair pushed away from the table, she straddled my lap, facing me, and pressed her forehead against mine, our noses touching. "Buddy," she said, and I reached under her housecoat and rubbed my thumbs along the inside of her thighs, and then there *were* explosions, millions of them, I thought, in that low place in my stomach. Millions and millions of them.

We'll take photos of your father's station wagon and of the Fisk and"—although she'd never been there—"a couple of shots inside your house."

We were sitting outside on the patio, our faces tilted toward the sun. The last snow was melting on the roof, and the thermometer behind us said sixty degrees, the warmest day all spring. I was letting Phoebe talk and I was listening.

"A picture is worth a thousand words," she said, and when she did I realized how much I'd always hated that phrase, but I ignored that part of me that still wanted nothing to do with recording my father's life on film, a life, I thought, worth more than any amount of stale words and snapshots. But I knew too that Phoebe was right, that even a glimpse of things at home would dissolve immediately any doubt about my need (that was the key word, need) for a scholarship.

So I started putting together in my head a kind of résumé I'd carry with me into the admissions office at Amherst, a résumé of disasters. I felt a little like a contestant for "Queen for a Day," ready to spill my guts, just like those three women on the TV each afternoon who believed in proper reimbursement for their years of deprivations, that fantasy—rags to riches. The audience always clapped and clapped each tragic history at the end of the show, the Applause-O-Meter's heavy needle struggling from left to right across the black-and-white screen. That was the strange thing, how adept the audience seemed at judging tragedy, determining a clear-cut winner on the spot, the queen for the day. Really it was for just a few minutes, that's all, at the very end of the show while she cradled a bundle of roses, breathed deeply this windfall of gifts with names like Tappan and Amana and Westinghouse. And the other two women, the losers? I figured they must have felt even worse, if that were possible, knowing that what they had told the whole world counted for nothing, their tragedies only second-rate, their suffering absolutely worthless.

Strange business, I thought, this handout stuff. "There's no such thing," my father would have said. "You'll pay somewhere, and you'll pay through the schnozzola." Maybe, but Phoebe had phoned Amherst and had set up an appointment that, the day after she left for Massachusetts, was confirmed in a letter to me from a Mr. Jeremy Snowday, the fellow in charge of all scholarships, the one who divvied up the money. I'd thank him graciously for anything he could do for me. That was all, just thank him. If Amherst wanted me badly enough, as Phoebe felt certain they did, I wouldn't be paying back any favors. This wasn't the mafia, it was college. And I trusted the sound of his name, Snowday, a sacred word around here each winter when the schools closed down. We didn't have to make them up, the missed days, I mean. They vanished forever like any other, but a guy felt lucky hearing "snow day" early some mornings on the radio. And there was something besides his name I liked too: I liked something he said, the tone he used. He referred to Phoebe in the letter as my "cohort." The deaf ear, the untaught, might have immediately thought crime, a cohort in crime, an accomplice. But I knew better—he meant only to be informal, signing his name fancy and big as life, and it was clear that he was anxious for me to meet him.

SEVEN

I couldn't carry much with me to the East Coast in the MGB—a couple of suitcases was all, the larger one wrapped in canvas and tied to the luggage rack. The trunk was stuffed full with a two-man tent Mr. Crouch had designed—a prototype, he called it, thinking that Phoebe and I might do some weekend camping and hiking and fishing in the Berkshires. I did manage to fit my fly rod and waders behind the seats (I'd read up on fishing native brookies and browns in Massachusetts and Vermont, in the Deerfield and Westfield rivers and farther north in the Battenkill), but what I wanted to do much more was drive to Pittsfield to search for Herman Melville's house, a different kind of fishing. I'd been reading "Bartleby," and Phoebe, in her American lit class, had just finished her semester studying *Moby-Dick*.

"I thought the book would never end," she had said one night on the phone. "Whales to infinity." I told her that last part, the whales to infinity, would make a terrific title for her final paper, but she said she'd already called it "On Melville." She did not find the kind of sanctity I did in the great books, but I hoped she'd be up for some literary travel anyhow—to Walden Pond perhaps, or up to Bennington,

Vermont, for some rubbings of Robert Frost's grave: *I had a lover's quarrel with the world.*

Me too, though my quarrel wasn't exactly with the world, not yet—it was mostly with my father's narrow vision of it. The morning I left Michigan he seemed subdued, tired of arguing, and he did not shout after me down the stairs. He just whacked his fist hard one time on the railing when I turned to say so long, to say without thinking the one thing that came into my mind, the one thing he could never have understood. I said, "I guess I'll be seeing you around."

I hadn't told him anything about Amherst College—or about the job waiting for me in Massachusetts. I'd write him after I got there and settled. Mr. Crouch had gotten me the job, though I'm not sure exactly how, halfway across the country. That sort of thing—ties, connections—had an order all its own. I assumed at first that I'd be working construction, a pick and shovel man, perhaps, breaking ground for a new power plant Mr. Crouch had had a hand in designing.

Not even close. I'd been hired, underage (you had to be twenty-one) and sight unseen, to drive a Ding Dong ice cream cart through the neighborhoods of Holyoke, the paper capital of the world and home of the birth of volleyball. Mr. Crouch seemed to know the city inside out. He said it had a system of canals that used to serve the mills, a second Venice for an architect with an ounce of vision. He said it also had a system of bars, one on every corner, "shots and beers." But I didn't care about any of that as long as they ate plenty of Eskimo pies and snow cones and fudgsicles. I could make a killing, Mr. Crouch had said, parking my cart (it was really a white truck) outside the main entrances to the mills, reading Dickens or Tolstoy until the shifts changed, and when they did I could turn my book over and ring the Ding Dong bell, a requiem to those tired workers.

I hoped my upbringing, my growing up poor, had taught me to meet these working-class people easily, to satisfy their simple desire for ice cream. I imagined I might recognize my father in each of them, the boredom and fatigue, the calcified stare behind their eyes. I didn't care that their eight or ten hours a day in the heat of those factories would profit me, the kid with the foreign books out to pocket some local money. I was confident they'd go ahead and order, and order regularly, five late afternoons each week, believing that some small part of me was struggling just like them, struggling desperately to get by.

Getting by I was, cruising in an MGB through Canada and upper New York State and down the Mass Pike to rendezvous with my girlfriend, maybe to be with her for good. I found Northampton and, from the directions Phoebe had sent me, I drove right to the house on Crenshaw. The funny thing was that I didn't park out front, not right away I didn't. I had a good station on, Dale and Grace singing "I'm Leaving It Up to You," which was worth a spin around the block even after driving a thousand miles, not to get my bearings exactly, but to take a few deep breaths of New England air at 6:00 A.M. and decide what it was I wanted to say, seeing Phoebe again after almost three full months. She wasn't expecting me until evening, but I was way ahead of schedule, making up, I thought, for years of lost time.

The apartment was on the second floor of a huge white house, black shutters, shrubs, and flowers everywhere. Phoebe had her own side entrance, and there was a fullness to the thick wooden stairs, new stairs, still unpainted, and they didn't creak at all when I climbed them. The screen door was unlatched, and I stepped inside.

Phoebe had done the apartment up right—potted flowers galore, succulents and lipstick vines and bridal veil all bunched in hanging pots, a canopy of color above the soft light of a single bay window. I wished Phoebe had been sitting right there waiting, a blanket around her shoulders. I would have knelt between her legs and rested my head in her lap and fallen asleep, prayerlike, while she massaged my neck, not a whisper to break the stillness. That's how I felt standing alone, spacey with love and tired too, but high on the energy of having pushed hard all night, each mile disposing more and more of my past. I didn't know if it was exhaustion or metamorphosis, but that other life seemed so long ago, seemed to be falling away. I tried to think of my father and I couldn't do it. And northern Michigan, that other country, was soil I didn't intend to trespass on anytime soon.

I liked the feel of my bare feet on the carpeted floor of my new apartment, and the way I looked undressing in the dark, full-length mirror on the inside of the bathroom door. Phoebe turned slowly over when I pulled open the covers and moved in close to her.

"It's you," she whispered, without opening her eyes, and I said, "Yep," and that was all, the back of her hand, knuckles and fingernails, already moving slowly and downward in tiny circles across my stomach.

I woke and sat on the edge of the bed, groggy still. I'd been asleep for almost thirteen hours, the shades drawn, door closed. I could hear sitar music on the stereo, and when I pulled on my pants and walked into the other room, Mr. Crouch's tent was erect—no pegs to bang into the ground, no ropes to tighten down. As he had explained to me, "It almost springs into shape on its own." Phoebe was inside, naked and in the lotus position on her sleeping bag, incense burning in a dish. Her legs were unshaven. I said, "Om," holding the long, sonorous O for a few seconds, and she slowly opened her eyes, not all the way, and she smiled and said, "All day I haven't been able to fly."

This was something new, the meditation. I hoped she wasn't fasting too, which she wasn't, and she said finally that she was hungry for dinner and, for almost two hours, in the back booth of the Miss Florence Diner, she gassed on and on about Baba Ram Dass and ashrams and the fleece of Himalayan llamas, about both India and China and how she needed (it was her summer's work) to transport her spirit out of the dark, cavernous echo of Western culture, that material consciousness.

We drank a lot of coffee, and Phoebe smoked half a pack of Winstons (another new habit), and I smoked a couple too, pretending to inhale, trying to minimize the distance between us, the "otherness" of our separate beings. She used lots of phrases like that, like "cosmic flow" and "energy centers," and she even quoted from the *Tibetan Book of the Dead*. It all went right by me. I was on another wavelength, and twitchy now from too much caffeine, and nervous about that interview scheduled the next morning with Mr. Snowday. I wanted to change the topic from "great space" to the Amherst College admissions office, from Sakyamuni, the Buddha, to me, a guy, not about to memorize sections from the *I Ching*, but rather the seven different flavors of Popsicles. To all kids I'd be Mr. Ding Dong. D.D., I thought, the flight and vision of a dodo bird.

Other people at the diner were eating hamburgers and

French fries (my order exactly) and someone in the booth right behind me mentioned Carl Yastrzemski, calling him Yaz at the instant Phoebe said Zen, the two sounds overlapping, *Yazzen*, and I tried not to smile, imagining the Buddha in the batter's box, his concentration perfect, eternal, but the baseball already by him, a third called strike, the essence of *thud*, deep in the catcher's mitt.

It was hard to hear the radio with the top down on the MGB and the muffler, which had just broken, rattling loudly, especially in third gear up the steep Easthampton Road. Phoebe pointed left, and I turned into the Mt. Tom Reservation, still climbing, downshifting now and stopping a few minutes later at the scenic overlook. We were the only car there and we were higher even than where I used to park at the bluffs.

"Wow," I said, turning the radio off and killing the headlights, then the engine. "Wow!"

All Phoebe said was, "Cigarette?" and I said, "Nah, no thanks," and I was glad, after she lit up, that the breeze carried the smoke behind us, away from my face.

"What river is that?" I asked, and Phoebe said back, "The Connecticut."

On the far side, what must have been miles away, the lighted windows of houses seemed to be blinking, the way I imagined a ship's windows would blink at night on the ocean, a kind of blueness rising. But I said none of that to Phoebe, who'd been getting more and more withdrawn. Twice she cleared her throat, as though she were about to say something, but each time she did not. Instead, she leaned her head back and closed her eyes, drawing hard on her cigarette and inhaling deeply, holding the smoke inside her lungs for a long time before blowing it out. After each drag she'd reach into the darkness beyond the car and flick her ashes, flick them hard enough so that the orange tip of the cigarette sparked. When finally it burned down almost to the filter, she sat back up and snubbed it out in the ashtray, which was already half-full of butts.

"Speaking of which," she said, "remind me on the way home to stop somewhere and buy another pack," and I thought, Speaking of nothing is more like it, because the truth was, we'd both gone closemouthed. We weren't talking about anything real, except in our heads, and I could feel the stir of irritation building, the way it does when it's past time for someone to speak frankly, to get what's bothering them off their chest. Phoebe's talk all day had been Zen talk, hocus-pocus, like so many things with her, a fad.

"Phoebe," I said, but I didn't finish—instead I picked out a single car heading north on the highway, a single car in heavy traffic, one of its headlights burned out, and I followed it, and although it was going maybe sixty miles per hour, it seemed like slow motion and without sound. And I thought then of silent movies, and how some weekend nights when I was much younger, my father would walk exhausted into the living room and turn down the volume so low on the TV that I'd have to try and read the lips of the actors, or move so close to the screen that I could feel the static on my clothes and on the fine hairs on my face. The only sound would be a thin crackling from the picture tube. And that's how the air felt here, electric and tense, like maybe a storm nobody knew about was close. I half expected to see lightning in the distance above the blinking red lights on a radio tower or smokestack or whatever it was jutting into the sky. But all I saw were stars, the Big Dipper and Orion and half a dozen other constellations I could have named, but didn't. I wanted instead to name this thing that was happening between us, and name it matter-of-factly and go from there. No gibberish, no lies, no worry about hurt feelings—just the truth.

"Phoebe," I said again, and she opened the door and got out and slammed it shut behind her.

"Damn you, Buddy," she screamed. "Don't make me say something I'll regret. Don't you make me—it's not fair!"

She stomped around to the front of the car, the whole time pointing through the windshield at me, pointing and screaming, "Damn you to hell, damn you, Buddy. Don't you come near me. Don't you dare come out here and touch me."

She stepped away, then toward the cliff, toward what I imagined was a sharp drop-off, hundreds of feet straight down. I could barely make out her silhouette, the dimmest white cottony outline of a ghost.

"Phoebe," I said, and when I hit the lights, there she was, her fingertips pressing her temples like she was lost or stunned. I could see she wasn't even close to the edge, and I don't know why, but I stared beyond her down the flood of the high beams and I remembered, whenever it snowed hard, how the heavy flakes seemed to rush into the headlight that was aimed too high, the left one. And always, after only a few minutes, I'd be straining and straining to see the road, expecting something or someone to be standing there in front of me. Which is what Phoebe was doing, shading her eyes now, her head tilted sideways and down.

I did not open the door—I pushed my whole body backward and up until I was sitting on the seat back; then I swung my legs over the side of the car and lowered myself quietly onto the ground. I did not walk toward her into the light, or circle wide and come up on her from behind. I'd spooked her enough already, so I simply waited there out of sight and, watching her, I realized she was a stranger as much as she was anything else at that moment in my life.

Below us the river and the cars were slogging by, though I didn't know where to. Specific places and times. And here I was on top of a mountain on June 6, 1965, a thousand miles from home. Not ten yards in front of me, my girlfriend frozen in the headlights of her own white MGB, the engine still ticking and cooling down. And I thought how each crazy detail was part of a series of reactions I did not understand, but of which I was the cause, the friction that ignited the spark that had started things colliding. Maybe it was something I'd said or left unsaid. All I knew for sure was that the next move was hers—the next word or gesture.

Which really didn't come until much later that night when Phoebe got out of bed to answer the phone after ten or fifteen rings—impatient rings, the kind you know won't stop for a while. I heard her say, "Hello," and then, "Hold on." She must have stretched the cord out to the landing because I could hear the screen door slap and then nothing. I imagined her sitting down on the top stair, the leaves of the maples turning silver under the stars. And I imagined her kind of knock-kneed, covering herself with her arms and elbows against the night.

She stayed out there a long time, and when she returned finally I pretended to be asleep. Whatever she wanted to tell me, I suddenly did not want to hear, not right then when my head was spinning. She'd preached earlier at the diner how the mind should be ever watchful, ever awake. Even to deception, I thought, but I wasn't about to force any conclusions about a guru boyfriend or anything else, not yet, not after what had happened at Mt. Tom. And not after the way she bent over me and kissed my cheek and stayed there staring a few minutes, inches from my face. I wasn't sure, but I think she was crying when she left, taking a pillow with her for the rest of the night, taking it into the two-man tent still pitched in the outer room.

Next morning the tent was down, and Phoebe wasn't doing her breathing exercises or declaiming "Dharma Combat" as the most enlightened human dialogue in the cosmos. She was fixing French toast and singing "Sweets for My Sweet" and when she spread a teaspoon of sugar on the small half globe of a pink grapefruit, she continued, "Sugar for my honey, I'll never ever let him go."

She was as thin as always, a little bony even, but her breasts seemed larger underneath the loose T-shirt she used as a nightgown, hanging just a little way down her thighs. I had never thought of an appetite swelling before, but mine was right then, not only for the food she was preparing, but for whatever flesh my tongue might touch—her neck or lips or the soft skin of her eyelids. And I got up from my chair at the table and, backing her against the kitchen counter, I held her close to me, because that morning in the kitchen, anxious and love starved and afraid of losing her, I had never felt such hunger.

There were no more late night phone calls after that, not a single one, and nobody showed up unannounced at the apartment. Phoebe cooled it on the Zen too, not dropping it completely (she'd still meditate now and then, usually in the bathtub while the water stayed hot), but expounding less and less the doctrines of Eastern thought and religion. She said she believed there was intelligence in a crow's caw or footprint—but that the combined mystical properties, billions and billions of them (just consider each grain of sand), was discipline for the bodhisattvas. And anyway, she said goal number one was to concentrate on the thousand dollars I needed to attend Amherst College beginning in September. That's what Mr. Snowday had told me at the interview. He said, "Figure on a thousand bucks and you're home free." Almost a full ride. That would cover books and room and board too. And Phoebe said she'd work with me for free some days in the Ding Dong cart if it would help, her atonement for having almost botched things between us. "I never slept with him," she told me. "I want you to know that, Buddy. It was more a spiritual thing."

I said simply, "We're okay now," and without a lot of promises and ultimatums we settled in for the summer, aware only of ourselves as a couple again.

E I G H T

I was paid on commission. "So you sell, sell, sell," said Leo Tomashek, a junior-high-school science teacher from Chicopee. "This is a good goddamn paying summer job. If it wasn't so seasonal, I'd drive Ding Dong all year long!" He told me he was forty-eight years old and had lit who knew how many Bunsen burners in his life. "From fire all school year," he said, "to ice."

"Robert Frost," I said, smiling, and he said back, "Horse manure, Robert Frost. Forget the poetry, my young friend, and remember, school's out. This, I hate to inform you, is the real world."

I trained with Leo for only one day, a scorcher, and he said, "Watch this," as we turned off the blacktop down a dusty two-track behind the weathered tobacco barns. "Here comes a quick thirty bucks." Then he started to teach what he called "lessons outside the classroom." He bent forward, kind of steering with his forearms, and he said, "This is what you're after, kid. Crowds. Baseball parks, parades. You don't care who they are, these people, who they've been with or where they live or anything else. You don't have to like them at all—there are mucho jerks out there, first-classers, who get off giving you crap, calling you Mr. Dong, pea brain, stuff like that. But they'll have money. Now pay attention."

He parked and rang the bell, though the migrants were already coming away from the fields, walking quickly in groups down the long rows, heads covered with red or blue bandannas against the sun. There must have been fifty of them, men and women and children, shouting together so fast in Spanish that I couldn't understand a single word, though I'd taken three years in school, conversational Spanish, and had even read sections of *Don Quixote* in the original.

"Point," Leo would say. "Point, point to it," and he'd lean forward through the large opening in the side of the truck to see what was being ordered and he'd say, as if to himself, the Spanish word for Creamsicle or Pushup, as though he were drilling himself with cue cards, memorizing vocabulary for an exam.

"Don't shortchange them on purpose," Leo said, "but if there's a gripe, remember the fault is theirs. They'll buy again next day, believe me. The heat out there would scorch a lizard."

When we got back on the main road, Leo said, "Go ahead—count it."

I did and then I said, "Thirty-two fifteen."

"Okay, lesson *numero dos*. Count how much we take in while we're driving, while we're en route." I looked at him, and he said, "That's right, zero. A smart boy like you ought to know what that means." And in case I didn't, he spelled it out. He said, "It means get your sweet ass to your next stop as fast as you can."

And that's the way the whole day went—drive, stop, drive, stop—and I was dead tired when we knocked off, about nine o'clock, right after the Little League games at Curtis Field let out. Back at the Ding Dong warehouse Leo showed me how to take inventory and restock and plug the truck in to keep the refrigeration going all night, and where to turn in the revenue for the day, that most of all. You left nothing in the cashbox, not a lousy dime. He seemed in no hurry to get home, though earlier he'd mentioned his wife, just that he had one. I had asked him then if he ever got to take her out to dinner. "You don't go out to eat if you're depressed," he said.

"Maybe you work too many hours."

"Not me," he said, "her. She's depressed. I love this job."

And he really seemed to, all of it, the pace, the long hours, and walking me over to my new rig that first night, he pointed and asked, "That yours?" knowing it was, and I nodded and said, "Number thirteen."

"You superstitious?"

"Nope," I said, and Leo swung his heavy arm around my neck and said, pulling me closer and talking into my ear, "Last fellow quit at noontime on his second day."

"I'll survive," I said.

"Good," Leo said back. "Good, good, good," pleased that he'd instructed me well. "It's good work," he said. "It's good money. Stick it out and you'll be farting through silk." I smiled, and he walked slowly away toward the parking lot outside, enclosed by a tall galvanized fence, his white uniform visible for a long time in the darkness.

I worked the next seven days straight, twelve-, fourteen-hour days, and took home $28.16, about 29 cents per hour for my first full week. The route I had stunk royally. The only ballpark was a skin infield behind a housing project off Kilmer Road, and the two times I pulled in there, the place was vacant except for one kid, a blond crew-cut kid, playing Fungo, hitting the badly scuffed ball and walking after it, slowly kicking up the dust. He came over holding his bat, a two-tone Louisville Slugger, the first day and asked, "You got anything for eight cents?"

"Not a single item," I said, and on the second day, from halfway across the diamond, he glanced up and flipped me the bird. He was nine, maybe ten years old.

The temperature had been in the nineties all week, high humidity, and Phoebe had had an air conditioner installed so the bedroom was nice and cool. We stayed awake one night talking, and I told her not to call her father, that I needed to make this job go on my own. "It's all location," I explained, "and the good money routes—the paper mills, tobacco fields, the construction sites—they all go to guys like Leo with ten years in. For me it's like shoveling fog. I ring and ring my Ding Dong bell through those sparse, middle-class neighborhoods and wait, like Leo told me, at the end of each block. And who shows? A couple of mothers, straggling out into the heat from their ranch homes, counting change as they walk toward me, pennies even, their children jumping up and down all excited, wanting this, no that, no this again. Could I please break the Popsicle in half? Good. Now, Jill gets the lemon side, Paulie the grape, et cetera, et cetera. And you know what I say? Do you? Honest to God, I say sure thing, sure I will, smiling the whole time, just like they're exactly the kind of customers I intend to keep happy and coming back again and again."

"Can't you stray a bit? I mean, that only seems fair, doesn't it?" Phoebe said.

"And if I happen to run into Leo or Del Convery or

someone? Or what do I say when those guys pull into the warehouse at the end of the day with only half a till and I'm in my truck already, counting up, miraculously, decent bucks for the very first time?"

"Then drive in a completely different direction, where there are no assigned areas."

"That's a major no-no, freewheeling, especially outside city limits. Out there you've got no insurance. Plus, I wouldn't have the vaguest notion of where to go."

"I would," Phoebe said. "Right to the overspill at the Leeds Reservoir, below the dam where I've spent the last full week working on this tan that you haven't even noticed, seeing me only in the dark."

It was true—Phoebe was usually in bed by the time I got home around midnight, and still sleeping when I left early the next morning. "I'm a Ding Dong widow already," she said, and she jerked the sheet from under her chin, all the way down past her waist, and reached over and switched on the three-way lamp to high. She had that deep olive skin that absorbed the sun so naturally, and she looked Polynesian lying there, her stomach flat and dark, her legs toned from all her biking. Had she gotten up and walked outside right then, I believe those large, white breasts would have glistened in the moonlight. I needed to siphon from them what I could—silence or disappearance—and I slid gently from one to the other and then, with my whole weight on top of her, we rocked back and forth, back and forth, our bodies pressing and pressing against each other.

The last thing Phoebe said that night was that people didn't really know themselves well without sex, that sex was a poultice, drawing the healthy part of each of us back into the world that mattered, the world we lived for, and that I should wake her anytime for that. "Don't hesitate," she told me. "I'll never say, 'Not now.' "

She wasn't kidding. We made love every night after that, and Phoebe stopped complaining about my job so much, which improved during week two. Nothing great, but I took home just under fifty dollars, nearly double my first paycheck. I knew the neighborhoods better now, which blocks to stop on and for how long. And the customers, kids mostly, got used to me arriving at a certain time and they waited for me, small change squeezed sweaty in their palms. During slow stretches, I thought about Phoebe. She seemed to be filling her days okay, though most of her friends from Smith had left the area for the summer. Only once did she get home to the apartment after me. She looked surprised to see me and said that she'd biked down to the Red Lion for some coffee and ice cream. "Buy from me," I said as a joke, but she pushed right by me into the kitchen for a glass of water, having pedaled hard uphill, I figured, panting against all that darkness.

Like me, Leo never took a day off, never, and he stopped by my truck on a Saturday night while I was restocking. One way to tell how sales had gone for a driver was by the pile of ice cream boxes he'd tossed out of the truck onto the concrete floor. Leo said, kicking them a little, "Not too dingy," and I said, "Want to trade?"

It was meant in fun, but Leo didn't take it that way. He said, "That's the big question, isn't it? Want to trade? Like it should ever be that easy. My route for yours? Not likely. How about my hair for yours?" Leo was half-bald and he was not smiling when he stepped up into my truck and sat down in the driver's seat, both his hands so tight on the steering wheel that his knuckles turned white, like phosphorus almost. As always, I had inched the nose of my truck up real close to the gray cinder-block wall, and that's what Leo saw, staring through the windshield, that wall and nothing else, as if he were speeding purposefully toward it.

"Lesson number whatever," he said, spinning around. "Take careful notes. What you learn here might just help to save you from yourself."

He sounded crazy, like my father did sometimes, a man given to paroxysms but fighting to stay calm, to keep the explosive world in check. As usual, Leo and I were the last two in the warehouse. I could hear the long, dull hum of refrigeration, that steady pulse lifting from the white line of abandoned ice cream trucks.

"Life's not like that, kid, swapping scrap for choice," Leo said. "Maybe after a few years you trade up—that's the best you can do, and you do it slowly, and only after the old route has worn you out, after you've paid your proper dues."

"That way is too slow," I said to Leo, and he said back, "Then why aren't you home like those others, like Convery and Lemcool and Carl Pavlich. How come, Buddy?"

"I'm leaving in a few minutes, after I clean up."

"But you'll be the first one back tomorrow morning," he said. "Won't you?" He paused and then he said, "Damn right, you will." And then, speaking more softly, he said, "Listen, it's not only money, kid. There's something else about this job you're learning to love."

That was nuts talk, pure weirdness, and driving home I felt sorry for the students who had to take his classes, a teacher with such a short fuse, dangerous, I thought, in a chem lab among fumes of sulfur. I remembered my father saying once, "It just plain stinks," and although I couldn't recall the context exactly, I knew the phrase fit here. It fit Leo and his lousy lecture on struggle, on the work ethic. I didn't buy any of it. I'd seen his act, the easy money (he made in one day what I did in a week), and if he had cultivated good business habits and strategies over years of summers with the migrants, it had been effortless. Sure, he'd memorized a few Spanish words for the merchandise he sold, but *gracias* was absent from his vocabulary, absent in any language. On that first training day, when I said thank you to a beautiful woman who had paid me with the exact change for two Dixie Cups (she was probably nineteen, twenty years old), Leo said, right out loud, "Never, never thank these people and don't smile at them either." Later I asked him why not, and he said, "Because that all costs extra, and I like to keep my prices down."

Leo's talk bugged me. Did he mean that he didn't kowtow to anyone now that he drove the primo route? Mr. Numero Uno? Mr. Long Dong of the Ding Dongs? Who needed it, these prolonged summer lectures. School was out, *o-u-t*. I had studied hard, and it had paid off big, *mucho dividendes*. Maybe I should have told Leo that, tweaked him a good one instead of having said, "Thanks for the advice," which is what he wanted to hear. I know, because he said back to me, and kindly, "Kid, you're very, very welcome."

That same night Phoebe said to me, "Too much sex is not enough." *That* kind of paradox made perfect sense, and we continued to go at it in bed pretty good, regular as clockwork. She said she understood how I needed to make the thousand dollars on my own, no gratuities, though in a pinch she could probably loan me however much I came up short—allowance money she hadn't spent. "I'll eke it out," I said, but I knew at this rate (I was up to almost sixty-five dollars a week) it would take me until the snow fell, coffee and doughnut season. I tried to be cheerful, positive. I said, "Better times approaching."

"They will if you become a surgeon," Phoebe said. "And I'll give you exactly eight years to do it, to get it done. Not one day longer."

That would be some haul, I thought, from Ding Dong to surgery at Mayo or Mass General, especially since I had no intention of entering medicine. I was hoping to become a writer, a poet, my books on somebody's shelves, like Manny had books on his shelves. But I played along, and I did like the metaphor, the symbolic distance covered by that dream—ice cream to glucose. And catch this—there was a blood drive going on in Northampton, which had started about the same time as my job. The Red Cross had erected, on the front lawn of city hall, a replica of a heart, a huge, clear plastic see-through, and every afternoon red dye, equivalent to the number of pints of blood donated, was poured in. Supposedly, when the goal was reached, the dye would begin to circulate through the heart's chambers, and it would actually begin to beat. So every night, coming slowly around the corner onto Main Street, and still dressed in white like an ambulance driver, I'd flash my high beams to inspect the heart's level. After three weeks it was still low, critical, the perfect gauge for the lifelessness of my job, its dim pulse. But I knew I could hang on if Phoebe could, if the job wasn't killing her or our relationship, which it wasn't, she said. She said we should think of all this time apart as convalescence that would only make us stronger and stronger, our lifeblood spilling over into the glory of the coming months and years ahead.

■ ■ ■

Leo said, "Convery called me a bloodsucker. I called him a whiner, a thumb sucker. You know I'm right."

I didn't know and I didn't care. I had Phoebe's transistor radio tilted on the open glove compartment door and I was listening to the Red Sox–Tiger game at Fenway Park, the second half of a twin bill. Detroit had been shut out in the opener, two-zip. I had planned to get tickets and drive down to Boston for the nightcap with Phoebe. Nothing real fancy—box seats along the first base line, a few beers and hot dogs, a bag of peanuts. But business had suddenly gone flat for everyone but Leo (he said migrants didn't take vacations). Convery complained that families were off to the Cape or to Misquamicut. It was late July, and I had saved only $260.00 and had given Phoebe nothing, not a red cent for food or gas for the car or for rent. Nothing, *absolutamente nada*. And I hadn't taken Phoebe out on a single date.

I hadn't bought her a present either. And I was sorry that I had ever mentioned Boston to her, only to back out of the trip. But she was terrific about it. She just got up on her tiptoes and kissed me on the lips and said, "I think you've gotten taller this summer," and that was all.

What could I say? She deserved more, and I decided right then, at the same moment Willie Horton singled in the go-ahead run in the ninth, that I'd head for the Leeds Reservoir the following afternoon, just like Phoebe had suggested weeks ago, to that crowded beach without a single concession stand. I'd surprise her there, laying eyes on her in the daylight for a change while she stretched out in the sun in her yellow bikini. So far I had only seen it hanging limp over the shower stall, damp and wrinkled. It was way past time to see her fill it out. It was time to make some money. Let my steady clientele (where were they anyhow?) whine for a while.

"Let them whine," I shouted over to Leo in his truck, and misunderstanding, he shouted back, "Not likely, needledick, not in your rookie season." And I flashed again on that beautiful woman from the tobacco field, and on the great Puerto Rican ballplayers, shortstops around the league who spoke little English and didn't need to, scooping expensive grounders, and who didn't know that migrant woman was even alive, waiting every day with the exact change for two Dixie Cups, paying quickly and walking away.

My mind had been jumping around like that a lot lately, from baseball to women to bits of conversations. And on my way home I kept thinking about that plastic heart, how the dye looked so dark at night in my headlights, dark like blood from something dead. Had I the time, I would have donated again and again. I wanted desperately to get that heart pumping—*ba-bump, ba-bump, ba-bump*—in time with my own, with Phoebe's, with this town where I hoped to settle down to a real life soon, all the vital signs steady, the healthy future in sight.

N I N E

Where the Leeds Road declined sharply, I stopped the truck and yanked back hard on the emergency brake and left the engine idling. Through the few straight rows of planted pines I could see the water clearly, and on the far side of the overspill where the lake widened, a boy suspended, turning backward gracefully in midair, the Tarzan swing's loose arc falling in slow motion away from his hands. His two buddies, sporting identical bright red bathing trunks, waited high on the embankment for their turn. By the way they stood, arms folded across their skinny chests, I could tell they were shivering, having been at this jungle wildness all morning. Below the dam, just beyond the spray, lots of people were sunning on the flat rocks, and farther down on the near side where the current slowed, small children squatted at the water's edge, playing with plastic shovels and pails, their mothers sitting on towels or blankets behind them.

It felt a little eerie to see a whole week's worth of potential customers in one place and nobody selling, not even a Kool-Aid or lemonade stand. Nothing. I coasted down, trying to locate Phoebe, my coconspirator, the real brains behind this wide detour, this single stop almost twenty miles outside my closest boundary. It wasn't like I was trespassing, mining somebody else's claim. This rich vein, as Phoebe had assured me over and over, had been abandoned, untapped all summer. The gold was there for the taking.

When I did spot her, I wished I had my father's binoculars because she was not alone. Some guy (he was kind of sideways to me so I couldn't get a good look at his face) was rubbing oil on the backs of her legs, rubbing it up and down a long time, more like a massage, from her ankles right to her rear end. I thought a couple of times that I saw his fingers slide under the edge of her bikini bottom. She was lying on her stomach, her face buried deep in the crooks of her arms as if she were asleep, dreaming. I rang and rang the Ding Dong bell, a kind of siren, and heads all over jerked up, Phoebe's among them, and she seemed startled as she reached real fast behind her back with both hands, clasping the thin strap of her bikini top.

I parked a little way back from the sand, and people bought and bought and asked if I'd stop by again tomorrow, and I nodded yes, sure, not so much at them as at Phoebe, who'd gotten up and combed her heavy, wet hair straight back from her forehead. I could see where the wide teeth of the comb had passed through. She looked beautiful standing there by herself, dark and thin and drinking from a GIQ (giant imperial quart) of Knickerbocker beer. When my last customer left, she walked over and handed me up the bottle by the neck and said, "Got room in your freezer to chill this?" I motioned her to come into the truck, which she did, a little tipsy, and she kissed me on the lips before I could push her away and ask, "Who's Joe Schmo on the blanket?"

"Who's who?" she said, and I said back, "You know who, the maestro with the magic fingers over there." He hadn't looked over at me the whole time. "Who is he, Phoebe?"

Her legs were oily, and when I stared down at them she did too. She never used Sea & Ski or Coppertone, no brand name drugstore tanning lotions. Instead she mixed her own concoction at home, part Johnson's Baby Oil, that clear liquid kind, and part iodine. It invited the ultraviolets, she'd say, those same rays that blistered so quickly the sensitive skin. Which is what she said I was being right then, overly sensitive and getting all burned about nothing. I lifted the bottle of beer in front of her face, not even sure how it was wrong that she should have it, when someone asked, "You selling that?" It was the kid from the Tarzan swing. His buddies were standing behind him, nudging each other, one of them giggling like a moron and turning away every couple of seconds.

"It's warm," I said.

"Warm's fine." He had goose bumps all over and he was maybe fourteen, tops.

"Them too?" I asked, meaning his buddies, and he said, "Yes, please," and I lined up three waxed paper cups and started pouring. They didn't balk when I charged them fifty cents apiece. The one kid just turned around and collected from the other two, and they each reached up and took a cup of beer and walked off away from where anybody was. As soon as they were out of earshot, Phoebe said, "The whole bottle cost only fifty-two cents."

"The trademark of the rich," I said, a phrase I'd heard my father use once, and before I could turn the conversation back to her friend, his back still toward us, those same three kids returned, more confident this time.

"Another round," the talker said, and even that did not empty the GIQ.

"Next one's on the house," I said, and all three of them

turned bottoms up and slapped their empty cups back down for the freebie.

"Thanks," they said. "We mean it, mister, really—thanks a million."

I couldn't talk to Phoebe the way I needed to with all the interruptions, and maybe that was good, giving me time to simmer down, though what I'd seen deserved no pretense of understanding. But, as Phoebe had asked, whose fault was this whole mess anyway? I'd been guilty all summer of too *little* conjecture, of allowing the days to pass and pass. Phoebe had obviously filled up the time with someone else. What did I expect, the world to be always waiting on me and my crazy Ding Dong schedule?

I was confused and I stared at Phoebe, close up, and her pupils were dilating, I guess from the beer and from having come all of a sudden out of the sun, and I thought, how easily the naked eye adapts to change, to all those variables of light and dark, those subtle gradations. And I'd been blind as a bat all summer (longer, more than likely) to Phoebe's obvious deceptions, and now, in the back of an ice cream truck, I was trying desperately to absorb the implications of each new moment, each breath and gesture from Phoebe, who started to sweat—we both did—immediately after I shut the service window and pulled down the shade, a CLOSED sign facing out. I'd never done that before, closed up shop, but some of the drivers did while they ate lunch or took quick inventory or rearranged stock in the freezer. "You want o-r-d-e-r," Leo had preached that first day, "so that when you reach in for an Eskimo Pie or a Bomb Pop you don't come out with a frozen banana or a Mars bar." He said that was true of life too. But I didn't think order mattered much to Phoebe, who opened one of the six freezer doors and slowly lowered her face into all that cold.

She stayed like that for several minutes, and I did not say anything and I did not touch the back of her neck, not right away, but when I did she reached over and opened another freezer door and another, the entire front row, and when she finally turned around her outstretched arms were smoking. And her face was smoking too and her neck. She held that crucified pose, eyes closed, while I reached around and unhooked her bikini top and let it fall to the floor. Then I took off her bikini bottom and unzipped my white pants. I remembered Leo saying, "From fire to ice," and I recited to myself Frost's doomsday poem. Something was coming to an end, that much was certain, and what I wanted right then was to disappear again into the rhythm our bodies always made together in bed. Those times redefined the world for us, its true order and balance, even when things were really out of whack. But this time it seemed like desperate sex, or worse, a quickie, me with my fly down, Mr. Ding Dong. And Phoebe knew it too, and there was nothing for her to do but get dressed, which she did, and I opened the service window for some air. Phoebe stared out and saw, and I saw, that her friend had gone, blanket and all, and where it had been spread out were two empty GIQs stuck upside down in the sand.

I said, closing the freezer doors, "Do you need a ride home?" At first she didn't answer me and then she said, without any edge of disguise in her voice, that he'd be waiting for her at the apartment.

"Inside?" I asked, and Phoebe nodded yes.

■ ■ ■

It was only five or six miles back to Northampton, and we didn't talk at all for a while, and strangely, that felt good. I drove slowly, and as we were passing the veterans hospital a couple of patients got up real fast from where they were sitting on the grass by a pond to flag me down.

"Don't stop for them," Phoebe said. "Please, not here. They're all shell-shocked and crazy and they won't have any money anyway."

"How do you know?" I asked, and Phoebe said, "Because the guy I was with at the reservoir works here three nights a week."

"He's a doctor?"

"No," Phoebe said, "he's kind of a guard. He does it for material for a novel he's writing."

So she was finally going to talk. I passed the two vets by and I imagined them locked in their rooms at night by this aspiring novelist who Phoebe said was real choosy about words. I asked her, though I don't know why, maybe in anger, if he liked the patients, and Phoebe said, "No, I don't think so, not from the chapters he's read to me."

"In bed?" I asked, and I immediately regretted having said that. Phoebe was quick to answer. She said, "Yes, sometimes in bed," and I knew my summer on the East Coast was over, and college too, at least at Amherst. After a few minutes Phoebe said, "I'm sorry," and I nodded, and whatever else might have been said was not said. When I stopped the truck to let her out in front of the apartment on Crenshaw, I asked her to get me my bankbook. She had been making my deposits for me every week.

"Okay," she said, "I will—I'll get it," and she crossed in front of the wide windshield, but I did not watch her go very far. I was exhausted and I lowered my forehead to the steering wheel and closed my eyes and didn't open them until she stepped back into the truck, five, maybe ten minutes later. She had changed out of her bikini and was wearing cutoff blue jeans, cut uneven and real short, and a sleeveless, Smith College T-shirt, and she had a string of brightly colored beads around her neck. She handed me the bankbook and said, "You owe me nothing."

"I know," I said, and I believed it. Then I said, "I'll bring back the MGB after work, and I'll get my stuff out."

"Where will you stay?" she asked.

"In the warehouse. For tonight, anyway."

She started to say something else, but I stopped her, saying, "Don't, not here," imagining that her friend was watching from the kitchen window, watching this thing end.

Phoebe stepped down onto the sidewalk and she started to cry, a strange kind of crying, lots of tears, but there was no sound, and her whole body stayed motionless, arms at her sides. She said finally, "Don't leave like this," but I did, and Phoebe took a few barefooted steps into the street and stood there. I watched her in the sideview mirror, getting smaller and smaller as though she were disappearing in a dream. After the curve I shifted into third gear and I did not look back.

I double-parked, like a Brink's truck, in front of the First National Bank, and I went inside to withdraw my savings. I had never closed an account before, and when the teller asked me how I wanted the money, I said, not meaning to be a smart aleck, "I want it all."

"What denominations?" she said.

I was confused, and there were people behind me, and I

said, "Catholic." A second teller glanced over at me and laughed, and I did too, a little, like it was a joke, but my teller saw nothing funny and started snapping new bills, mostly twenties, in front of me on the counter. Then she stamped, in red ink, VOID across the face of my bankbook and slid that to me and said, "Next." I left the bankbook right there and walked away, folding the bills, and casually, as if it were a pack of cigarettes, I stuffed that wad of money into my shirt pocket.

My mind was racing, and I don't know, maybe just to focus on something that felt good, I remembered, on my way out of the revolving glass doors, how my father joked once that he was so broke he couldn't pay attention. Funny I should think about that coming out of a bank, but I did. And I remembered how he had said it, softly, like it was a big secret, to the new checkout girl at the IGA. She played along, holding out both her hands (she had long, thin fingers and no rings) while my father counted out quarters and dimes and pennies, the last of his change before payday. He was buying a six-pack of Stroh's. She smiled the whole time, even though he was broke, and I knew that mattered a lot to him. On the way out to the car he paused and glanced back at her through the thick, plate-glass window and then, walking into the parking lot, he winked at me.

I might have been searching for a similar connection when I stopped at a package store in downtown Holyoke. The building was covered with ivy, except around the windows and door and where it was neatly trimmed to expose a thermometer to the early afternoon sun. Already the thermometer read eighty-five degrees.

A bell jingled when I opened the door, and I nodded hello to a white-haired guy behind the counter. He was short, and looking down at him I felt old enough to buy beer and I took my time checking the fancy imported labels in the cooler behind him: Guinness Stout, Dos Equis, McKewin's Scotch Ale. But when I ordered, I asked for a single Piels, a local beer.

I liked the sound the cooler door made as it clicked open, then closed. He hadn't asked me for an I.D. He only said, "Will that be it?" and without hesitating I said, "And four more cases, returnables."

"Thirteen ninety-six plus a single, fourteen twenty," he said, adding it in his head and handing me a couple of bottle openers before walking into the back room.

He was running a sale on Piels, $3.49 a case. The brewery was only a few blocks away, down by the canals. I had passed it once, on the beginning of a long route I took home one night through the surrounding towns: Holyoke, South Hadley, then over the Notch to Amherst and finally back to Northampton, to the apartment, to Phoebe already asleep.

A mirror hung eye level to me on the wall beside the counter. The sign above the mirror said Now TELL ME AGAIN YOU'RE 21! I was eighteen, illegally driving Ding Dong and now stocking alcohol I hoped to sell to all the minors I could. My father would have said, "Don't do it," but I was all done working for peanuts and I was all done mooching from Phoebe and from the Crouches and from all the Mr. Snowdays, who didn't mean to, but diminished nonetheless the worth of a person's life. I had paid plenty, as my father told me I would, and I figured whatever debt I had with any of them was canceled, and if I could, I'd pad my wallet for the trip home to northern Michigan with some easy money.

I held open the front door for the guy as he pushed the dolly outside to the truck. He handed each case up to me through the service window, and I stacked them on the floor and paid him with exact change from the cash drawer. He was sweating right through his shirt, and I said, small talking about the heat, "At least it's good for business."

"For you," he said. "I'll take winter anytime. My markup's on the hard stuff." He paused, catching his breath, and then he said, "Figure it out—how much profit can you squeeze from a case of Piels?"

I wasn't sure, but I figured a lot if I could find a ballpark, which I did about twenty minutes later, a huge park called McKensie Field. It had three baseball diamonds, the outfields converging so that I imagined players on different teams standing back-to-back, just a few feet apart. I wondered if they talked out there during league games, talked without ever seeing each other's faces. Or if they ever collided, chasing deep drives, and if so, how that would be scored.

Nobody was in uniform—all pickup games. No coaches, no adults in the hot bleachers. So I pulled right behind a backstop. The catcher, getting up from his crouch, turned toward me and said, almost apologizing, "Good Humor just left, not ten minutes ago."

"I've got ice-cold beer," I said, and he threw off his mask as though chasing a foul ball, dropped his mitt in the dust behind home plate, and was first in line. With the room from all the ice cream sales at the reservoir, I fit three and a half cases of long necks in the freezer, and I sold them all, one dollar apiece, some kids loaning money to their friends. There was some chatter about cops, and someone kept calling Piels weasel piss, and one kid, coming in late from deep right, pointed up at me and said, "You're crazy—do you know that?" And to the others, "I don't want any part of this," but he got shouted down, guys yelling "Screw you," and "Up yours," and making threats about him saying anything to anybody about the beer. They were all older than the Tarzaners at the reservoir, maybe fifteen or sixteen. The kid who wasn't drinking calmed down finally and ordered a cherry slush, which I gave him free with lots of extra syrup.

"The cops, they patrol here all the time," he whispered. But already the players were heading out to their positions, and although they were loud and laughing and grabbing one another in headlocks, I'd collected all the empties and put them in the cases and restocked the freezer with the remaining twelve beers.

"Thanks for the warning," I said, and he headed out in the other direction, away from the game, which he said I had ruined. Maybe so, but when I passed him a few minutes later on the road, I rang my bell, and he waved, waved without looking up, by raising his glove hand, the cherry slush held tightly, like a deep drive he had just snagged, in the stiff webbing.

Between the Leeds stop and McKensie Field and heavy ice cream sales at the entrance to Whiting Paper Company, I had earned a bundle, almost three hundred dollars. It was six-thirty, and there were at least two good hours of light left, and none of the other drivers were back at the warehouse. It felt strange to knock off so early, my truck restocked, the refrigeration plugged in for the night. There was nobody to come around to chat, but I locked the truck up anyway, and on the floor, right under the interior light, I divided the Ding Dong money from the Piels money, and what was mine I took in bills and added it to that wad I had carried all day in my shirt pocket.

Lynette Wallaker, the cashier in the office, knew to the

penny how much each driver made—daily, weekly, and for the entire season. Lemcool, who tried to flirt with her a lot, said to me once that she was single and hot to trot and whoever won Chief of Sales for the summer also got to war dance in her bed. Carl Pavlich, who was standing there, said, "Lemcool, you'll die with a hard-on," and Lemcool, looking from Carl to me, said, "Then the gravediggers will have to go down an extra ten inches," and he laughed, and so did Carl, but I just shook my head.

"Chief of Sales," he said again when I started to leave, "and the bonus is a boner for Lynette."

I liked Lynette a lot, so I stopped and turned around and said to Lemcool, as sarcastically as I could, "And of course you'd know."

"Perfect-o change-o," he said. "Once a year, baby. Once every frigging year."

Lemcool had good sales—I knew that. He drove Forest Park, the Springfield Zoo, but he didn't push the day the way Leo did. I asked Leo later who'd won Chief of Sales, and he said he had, six years running, which is about what I'd figured. Then I asked him about that war dance stuff, and he said, shaking his head, "Lynette wouldn't give you savages, any of you, the time of day."

But she had, to me anyway, the low man on the totem pole, and some nights, when we were the only two still there, she'd talk on and on, about nothing, really. And several weeks back she had given me a key to lock up, even though she was supposed to be the last one to leave, no matter how late that was. I had promised never to mention the key to anyone, never. I had driven her home once, too, the top down on the MGB, when her VW wouldn't start.

"Your car?" she asked. I said, "Yes," and I remembered

how that lie felt all wrong and how she rested her bare arm on the back of my seat, and how the tips of her fingers brushed my neck as the car bounced on that stretch of Appleton that was still cobblestones. Before she got out, she waited a few minutes, staring straight ahead, then she looked at me and said, "I'm thirty-one," and then she invited me into her house.

I was thinking about that and about Phoebe and how I was still glad I hadn't gone into Lynette's, but wondered now if I could stay there for a few days if I needed to, just to sort things out. And that's what I went down to the office to ask her. I hadn't even brought the day's paperwork or the money with me.

I walked up close to the cashier's window, but she didn't hear me, her back turned, and I could see her bra straps through the white blouse, and how one of her high heels was kind of hanging by her toes as though she might kick it off under the desk. I stayed maybe two minutes, then backed away, slowly at first; then I turned and ran as fast as I could down the hall, not back to my truck, but outside to the parking lot, where I hoped the MGB would not be boxed in by Lemcool or by Stapleton, who always left work way before I did. If I had to, I believe I could have pushed their cars out of the way by hand. But there was room for me to squeeze by, which I did; then I wound through the gears onto Route 9, a straight shot to Phoebe, who had to be waiting for me, had to be, for the kindness and patience and love it would take to make things right again between us.

The apartment was dark. I walked through it and turned on the bedroom light. My extra Ding Dong shirt and pants were hanging on my side of the closet, right next to the dress-up clothes I had brought with me from Michigan for my interview at Amherst. I hadn't worn them since. My waders were in there too, folded over my suitcase. I slid the closet door closed.

Phoebe and I had made love before I left for work that morning, and although she had tidied up the room some, the pillow she had slid under her rear end was still in the middle of the bed. The room was cold, the air conditioner whining full blast, so I switched it off, then the light, and at the window I watched the moon, almost full, above the Smith College campus. I had been over there only once, two days after I arrived. We had walked around all morning, holding hands, Phoebe showing me the dorms and the art building and the path around Paradise Pond, the river flowing slowly in. We crossed a bridge to the athletic fields where she said she had played field hockey all spring for her gym requirement, and beyond the fields, across a paved road, she pointed out the long white stables. She had said, "That's where the Smithies keep their Thoroughbreds."

I had never been on a college campus before, and I liked this one, especially the greenhouse, which Phoebe saved for last. We stayed inside a long time, breathing deeply the fragrance of all those exotic flowers. Phoebe had her favorites, and if she thought I sniffed one too quickly, she'd say, "Closer," and I'd touch my nose to the delicate corollas. When we came outside, Phoebe said, "Do you feel dizzy, like you're a little drunk?" and I said, "Yes," intoxicated, I thought, by the promise of exchanging my old life for all this. But Phoebe said, "It's the nitrogen—it gets you high."

"Like good wine," I said, and she said back, "And without any aftertaste or hangover."

We started walking back home then, walking and kissing and laughing all at the same time, tipsy with love, so perfectly drunk that I whispered to Phoebe, extending the metaphor, "Never a moment's abstinence."

"Not for two lushes like us," she said, and we stumbled on purpose for a few steps and then again, crossing Elm Street, right after a funeral passed—the shiny black hearse and the line of black Cadillacs that followed with their lights on. Even that could not sober us up, nor could that woman who lifted her veil and stared at us as if to say, "You'll see— you'll see soon enough."

I thought I'd go walk the campus again. I visualized Phoebe there alone, crying, or maybe having cried herself to sleep in the long grass. But I got only as far as the stairs and sat down, the way my father always did on Saturday nights, smoking Pall Malls and gazing up at the stars. Other than the Big and Little Dippers, he couldn't identify the constellations, and when I tried one night to name and point them out, one after the other, he said, "Whoa, slow down, slow down. Just sit with me."

I was angry that he'd cut me off like that and I stayed only a few minutes, saying nothing to him as I left. Now here I was, staring up into that same immense silence without any need to claim the stars. I watched them a long time, and when I finally went back inside, it was to pack my suitcase. I dropped the car keys on the kitchen table, on top of a note I wrote saying I'd send for my fishing pole and waders once I got settled back in Michigan. In case she wanted to get hold of me before I left, I jotted down the number of the pay phone in the Ding Dong warehouse. I had to get the number from information. I said in the note that I'd be able to hear the phone ring—it wasn't too far from my truck—and for her to call anytime, underlined, exclamation point.

I hadn't eaten anything since breakfast. I wasn't hungry exactly, though my stomach was growling, and I knew I should get a little food down—a glass of milk at least, or a couple of pieces of sliced ham. I opened the refrigerator. At eye level were two GIQs, one half-empty. For a couple of seconds I wanted to smash both bottles in the sink and leave, just get out. But I didn't. Instead I took a few long belts, pressed the rubber stopper back on, and slid the GIQ back on the shelf. Phoebe always kept the refrigerator dial on nine, half-freezing things, so the beer was very cold and tasted good. I didn't know if they'd notice it gone. I hoped not. I had left everything else in the apartment the way I'd found it, everything except the pillow. I had already moved it back to the head of the bed.

It was just past midnight, and I was standing under the huge clock on city hall. The blood drive had gone over the top earlier in the week, and that clear plastic heart was pumping away, valves opening and closing. I had only seen it from a distance and had never heard the artificial blood splash through the tubing like that into the heart's different chambers. I located my pulse and pressed my thumb there on my wrist. I'd been born with a heart murmur, but I felt no irregular beat right then, just one that was out of sync with the larger rhythm of this town, the life I had only imagined existed for me here. I picked up my suitcase and I cut across the grass, running now, then diagonally across Main Street to the intersection, and stuck out my thumb. The very first car stopped, then squealed its tires backing up. I don't think

I could have stood a slow ride to West Springfield, or a lot of conversation, and this kid, out cruising all alone, did not disappoint me. He only said, "Where to?" and I told him, and on that stretch of road by the Oxbow, just before the Easthampton line, he hit one hundred miles per hour. I relaxed right then for the first time all day, closing my eyes and listening to the music the tires made, reaching those nearly impossible high notes that might have shattered a wineglass, had I been holding an empty one in front of me in the darkness, trying hard but finding absolutely nothing to toast.

He dropped me at the entrance to the warehouse and headed right back in the direction from which he'd come. From the empty parking lot I watched his taillights, the glass on one of them broken, until I couldn't see them anymore. I was holding the key Lynette had given me, the one to lock up with. Supposedly, it activated the security system, so I assumed it did the opposite too, automatically. She hadn't ever mentioned if the alarm was silent or not.

I had never sneaked back in like this before, never, and it made me nervous. But I turned the key in the lock, and the door opened, and when I got back to where the trucks were lined up, I stood there, listening to the steady hum of refrigeration until my eyes adjusted some to the dark. I didn't expect the phone to ring, and if it did, I wondered if I could find it by following the sound. Some guys called out on it, but I had never heard a single call come in. Usually Lynette took messages on the office phone and gave them to the drivers as they cashed out. This was the first time I hadn't done that, cashed out. The ice cream money was still locked in my truck. Sometimes drivers got sick on the job and held on to their cash an extra day or two, but it was a lousy policy,

Leo had lectured me back in June. He said it made thieves of us, and that's exactly how I felt walking slowly through the warehouse, as though I intended to dump out my clothes and fill the suitcase with cash from all the tills.

And that must have been what the police thought when they arrived. I could hear car doors closing and some talking outside, then someone on a megaphone, saying not to move. I didn't, and when the ceiling lights blinked on, I let go of my suitcase and raised my hands above my head. After what seemed like long minutes, two cops stepped out, one from each side of Lemcool's truck, which was directly across from me, their guns drawn and aimed at me. They steadied them with two hands, just like the cops on TV. Then there were more cops, maybe three or four of them, and one yelled, "Get on your stomach." Then much louder and meaner, "And push your face into the floor, you punk," and I did that too, my heart beating faster and faster beneath that thick wad of bills still folded in my shirt pocket.

I sat alone in the backseat of a cruiser, its blue light slapping hard against the aluminum side of the building. The cops hadn't said anything about me selling beer at McKensie Field, and they hadn't searched my truck or even asked which one it was, though they had already been through my suitcase a couple of times, and through my wallet, and they had frisked me and found my money and didn't believe I had closed my savings account that afternoon, leaving the canceled passbook at the bank. I knew my story sounded lame, but I kept insisting like crazy that it was the truth and that I'd never stolen anything in my life and never would, and when I was just about to cry, one cop took charge, saying to the others, "Let me talk with him alone."

I was glad when they walked off a ways, and he said to me, "I'm Officer Dorociak." He acted too sullen, and it made me nervous the way he kept flicking the tip of a toothpick, as though he were trying to light a stick-match with the back of his thumbnail. But at least he hadn't sworn or yelled at me or threatened me like the others had, and although he was the one who smelled beer on my breath and had made a big deal about it at first, he had also defended me, saying to the other cops who had wanted to haul me right down to the station for interrogation, "The kid's not drunk. Just hold on—hold your horses a minute."

I guess he knew that by the way I answered all the questions without hesitation or without stumbling over a single word. I remember, when we were alone finally, how he flipped the toothpick right past me, watching where it landed, and how he stepped closer and tugged the sleeve of my uniform between his finger and thumb and said, "I believe you work for Ding Dong. What I can't get straight is why the hell you're here so late, all packed up to leave for someplace with all this cash." He held it up in front of me, kind of shaking it as though he meant to toss it right in my face. Then he said, "Give me a name, someone I can call who can help you out."

"Lynette Wallaker," I said, and I explained who she was and all about the key and locking up late, and while I talked Officer Dorociak turned me around and undid the handcuffs and followed me to the pay phone, which I hoped and hoped would not ring.

It didn't, but Lynette's rang for a long time, and no one answered. I thought right then about that night I drove her home and how she had kept one of her fists pressed between her legs to keep her skirt down in all the breeze.

"Strike one," Dorociak said, and taking his time he lit a cigarette and raised his eyebrows like, "What's next?" and I started in about Amherst College and how my girlfriend attended Smith and now that everything had collapsed between us I was going back home to Michigan.

"Well?" he said. "She got a name?"

"Phoebe Crouch," I said, but I wouldn't give him the number or tell where she lived unless he promised to let me make the call in private and talk to her for a few minutes first.

"Okay," he said. "Okay, but you'll make that one from the station." Then, walking behind me out of the warehouse, he repeated, perhaps so he wouldn't forget it, Phoebe's name a couple of times. He said, "Phoebe Crouch, Phoebe Crouch," and I closed my eyes, listening only to that sound.

Sometimes, when my father felt surrounded or ganged up on, he'd say, "Time to dismount and shoot your horse." I felt that way, outnumbered, and I felt a terrible loneliness as I climbed the front stairs of the police station, a huge, gray stone building. The cop behind the desk did not even glance up as I was escorted in, just another petty criminal, another dumb-ass kid in hot water. The cop was fat bellied and a lot older than Dorociak, and his face appeared featureless, chalk-like, almost ghostly under those fluorescent lights. One eye kept blinking and blinking, and I wondered if that was deliberate, a kind of Chinese water torture, that and the TV, which was mostly static. The desk cop wasn't watching (he was reading a magazine) though he was facing the TV, his feet crossed on a green vinyl ottoman. Officer Dorociak said to me, "Sit down," and I did, on a long bench, reserved, I thought, for exposing our very weakest selves.

I expected Dorociak to return, but he did not. I was tired and hungry and I put my head in my hands, elbows on my knees, and after a little while I must have drifted toward sleep. The desk cop, standing over me, startled me awake. He said, "One call," and handed me a pad and a pencil. I wrote down Phoebe's phone number, which he explained I'd give to him after he signaled me over. He'd dial while I held the receiver to my ear. But he was in no rush—he'd make me wait some more. I got up and moved a few steps to the watercooler and pressed my foot on the pedal and waited until the water turned cold. Then I drank, the whole time staring at the bulletin board plastered with profiles and head-ons of rapists and kidnappers and murderers, all on the FBI's most wanted list. And whenever the electric fan rotated by me, the bottoms of those posters would lift a little bit away from the wall in the breeze.

I had this sudden urge to turn around and explain to whoever would listen how my father, years ago, ended up in jail once overnight, not that he was dangerous, not really. And although he'd never been fingerprinted, they watched him closely after that for weeks. He spent the days inside, going from one window to another, staring out, as though he were under house arrest. And those nights he'd talk to me. He'd come right into my bedroom and touch my hair and face until he thought I was asleep, and sitting on the edge of my bed, he'd turn away, probably thinking about what he'd said to me or hadn't, or how certain words must have sounded like lies, simple words he had used, words like "future," or "grateful," as in "for what we had," which, I later learned, was very little, barely enough to survive.

I wanted to cross out Phoebe's number and write ours down, and I almost did, heavy black numbers, just so I could hear my father's voice. I wouldn't even mention the pickle I was in, and talk instead about regular things—the riga-marole of work at Ding Dong, how the long hours had gotten to me pretty badly lately, and how I was really anxious to get home, maybe fish with him again and relax some before school started in Ann Arbor that fall.

I hadn't spoken to him a single time the entire summer, and all I'd sent him was one postcard, and that was back in June, a postcard of Ernest Hemingway holding two enormous rainbow trout on the bank of some river in Sun Valley, Idaho. I had found the black-and-white postcard in a used bookstore in Amherst on the day of my interview. That seemed a long time ago, but I remembered wishing that the fish had been caught in the Big Two-Hearted, water my father trusted, northern Michigan water. And I remembered jotting down something safe and predictable on the back, something like, "Arrived safely—weather's good. Start job tomorrow," in-stead of what I had really wanted to say, which was, "This man who killed himself was so happy on that day in 1939. Look how he smiles into the camera. Look at the size of those fish!" But I steered clear of those touchy subjects, sad-ness and suicide, with my father, and I would have again on the phone, had I called him.

But at 3:00 A.M. I knew he'd be working at the Fisk, and I thought about that and how he once told me, right out of the blue while I was cleaning and oiling a Mitchell reel at the kitchen table before season, how much he liked to save his last cigarette break and take it alone in the predawn, just outside the factory door, even in winter. I imagined him shivering and exhaling smoke from deep in his lungs, smoke he'd contain a long time before releasing it into the frigid air. I never understood how the solitariness of those quirky few minutes could matter so much to him, but they did. That was the strangest thing about my father, how he could be so peaceful at the oddest times, and at other times, berserk in his madness.

Although I hadn't inherited my father's temper, I felt at that moment that I could go either way, all depending on what Phoebe said, how she reacted. But she didn't say anything, not at first, because it was her boyfriend who answered the phone. He said, "Hello," and waited, and then he said it again. Then it was Phoebe on the phone, sounding half-asleep, and she asked, first thing, if it was me on the other end, and I simply looked up at the desk cop as if the phone was still ringing, and he shrugged his shoulders, and I hung up.

"You got someone else to call?" he asked. "Your mother or father? They'll find out sooner or later."

"No, they won't," I said. Then I said, "My mother's dead," and when I did, I missed her more than I ever had in my whole life. I started to cry, and using all my effort to stop, I couldn't. After a few minutes he touched my shoulder and he said, "Are you hungry?" and I wiped my eyes and said, "Yes, I really am."

He pulled the phone directory from behind the desk and flipped back through the yellow pages and wrote a number down on the pad, right under Phoebe's. He dialed, as he had before, using the eraser end of the pencil, but he did not hand the receiver to me. Someone answered, and he said, "One Papa C's Deluxe, a medium." Then he said, "Hold on," and he looked right at me and asked, "You like anchovies?" and I nodded yes. "Yes," he said into the phone, and that was the one word I remembered most from the whole night. It's what I said when he came in to my cell to ask if

I was okay and to take away the pizza box and 7-Up bottle. "Yes," I said, sitting on the edge of the bed, and he said, "That's good," in a way he never would have to a dangerous suspect, locked up, ignored in every way possible to make him feel even more guilty, more guilty and absolutely alone.

T E N

"Holy jumping Jehovah," Leo said on our way out of the police station the next morning. It was already ten o'clock, and he was dressed for work. "The cops got hold of Lynette at home, and she calls me, and my wife tells her, 'Hold the phone,' and gets me out of the shower. I'm dripping wet and I can't believe what I'm hearing, that you're in the slammer, arrested for breaking and entering, all because you had no place to stay? You, Mr. College Scholarship on his way to stardom, can't figure out a place to stay? Why didn't you call me?"

"It's more complicated than that, Leo."

"No, it's not," he said. "It's simple—it's the girlfriend, and the girlfriend's turned you into a nobody."

I didn't answer, and Leo said, "Get in the truck," which I did, after he stepped up, and I tipped my suitcase on its end, using it for a seat. He drove a ways without saying anything, and then, glancing over at me, exaggerating his disgust with a slow double take, and then another one, he said, "You look like hell. Your uniform's filthy."

"I've got a clean one with me," I said, and he seemed pleased by that until I said, "But who cares?"

"I do," he said, "and about your hair—it's too damn

long—and because you're working for me today, you have to care too. That's your sentence. You work with me, you look the part. You look the part, you sell ice cream. Nobody buys more than once from a slob." The whole time he lectured me, he jabbed his right index finger into the air between us, and when he stopped once for a red light, he leaned over and jabbed me three quick times on the shoulder, pretty hard, and his lips were pursed real tight, and I thought he might slap me then, but he didn't. He just drove, both hands pinching the steering wheel, and I went into the back of the truck to change. And strangely, it did feel good to get out of those clothes I'd slept in, and into something cleaner, the ones Phoebe sometimes ironed for me.

I thought of her doing that, spraying the shirt with water from a bottle, then sliding the hot iron up and down the sleeves, across the collar, down the front between all the buttons. I knew how to iron—I'd done it for years—but Phoebe, earlier in the summer, had said she wanted to, and did, maybe half a dozen times before she quit for good, deciding instead to sleep in.

When she had ironed early those mornings, she always did it naked, as though those were the clothes she meant to slip into for the day. But only once did she wear my Ding Dong shirt, my name (although the letters were frayed) stitched in red across the pocket, and that was the morning a chickadee flew into the windowpane she was staring through while the iron heated up. She told me later that she felt the bird's neck snap on her forehead, which was pressed against the cool glass. I didn't know if that was true or not. What was, was that she put on my damp and wrinkled shirt and held the front closed as she hurried down the back stairs. The shirt opened when she reached for the bird in the grass.

The whole time it took her to climb back up, I watched her breasts, and from my angle above they seemed so white and full in the first light. I had never seen her more beautiful, a single barrette holding her hair out of her face, her heavy breathing seeming so loud above that tiny dead bird cradled in both her palms.

"Better," Leo said, "much better," when I came back up front, and he handed me an unsealed envelope, a crease down the middle where it had been folded in half, TRUCK #13 typed in red in the upper left corner as though it were a return address.

"Lynette unlocked your truck and closed your books herself, and she sent you this, your final paycheck."

Lynette had taken inventory, figuring the amount exactly. Paper clipped to the check was a note, which I wondered if Leo had read. It said,

> *Best not come by. Beer bottles taken care of. Axthelm here and nasty. I mentioned nothing about giving you that key!!! It would mean the noose for me too. Think about my place for the night. L.W.*

Axthelm was the owner and he almost never came around. I had talked with him only once, and he said to me back then, "I'm Mister Axthelm. Heavy on the Mister, heavy on the Ax." I thought at first he had said, "Heavy on the mustard," as though he were sending me out to the deli for a ham and swiss on rye. "Okay," I said, and smiled, but he wasn't friendly back. Instead he said again, but this time more slowly, enunciating each word, "Heavy on the Mister, heavy on the Ax." Spoken like that, it sounded like a warning, an either/or ultimatum. So Mr. it was, and until last night I had avoided the Ax. I figured if Axthelm didn't find out about the beer, he'd cool down and probably wouldn't press charges, and I could leave Massachusetts without a criminal record, which was important to me because I knew a record could follow a guy his whole life. My father had told me that, how the law was conspiratorial, letting you go but never letting you out of sight, never really leaving you alone, which was all I wanted anymore, to be left alone so I could make tracks and recover from this whole mess back home.

"The Greyhound leaves for Detroit at seven-fifteen tonight out of Springfield," Leo said, as if reading my mind. "You've got someplace to go until then?" he asked sarcastically.

I said, subdued, "You know I don't," and he said, "Dumb, dumb, dumb. It's a good job you threw away."

"Not for me, Leo. It wasn't good, it didn't pay, and you know I worked hard as anyone."

"Harder!" he said. "You worked harder than anyone, but you didn't listen to me, not good enough you didn't. I told you that first day it would be no picnic, but that it would produce eventually, a year, two years down the pike. This working for a living isn't a crapshoot!"

"No," I said, "it's not a crapshoot, it's just a lot of crap."

"Crap happens," Leo said, and I thought about that and I knew it was true. Perhaps that's what I'd come all this way to find out, a lesson my father had tried to teach me for years, how uncompanionable the rich and poor turn out to be, and how the poor travel finally away from desire, settling for what is, the crap that happens.

"And that's okay," Leo said. "That's the world." He hit his blinker then and slowed for the entrance to the Providence Hospital.

On the huge and very green lawn sloping all the way to Riverdale Road was a sign advertising the CHANNEL 22 TELE-THON. There were fat black cables stretched across the pavement on the side parking lot, and there were two TV cameras and booths everywhere, some under red and white canopies, and under those the Candy Stripers were selling Saint Christopher medals and scapular medals and pocket Bibles, all proceeds going toward construction of the new children's wing. I had heard some of the guys at work saying that Axthelm was sending a truck over (he wanted to cash in on the free TV coverage), but nobody knew who it would be.

Leo parked next to a long barbecue. The edges of the briquettes were white, but the chicken was not on the grill yet. Wings and breasts and thighs (what my father always called "chicken pieces") were stuck together, pink and heavy-looking inside clear plastic bags, big ones, bags half-submerged in a tub of ice water. A sticker on the tub said POULTRY EXPRESS.

"We're in good shape," Leo said. "Things are just heating up." He unwrapped a root-beer barrel and kind of squeezed it from the cellophane into his mouth, and when he turned, still in his seat, to talk to me, he slurred his words like he was drunk. But I understood him. He said the telethon wouldn't amount to a hill of beans with building costs the way they were. And he said not to worry if the TV camera stopped on me, because Axthelm wouldn't know me from mud and he wouldn't be watching in the first place. "He owns Ding Dong," Leo said, "and he makes a ton of money off it, but he doesn't know beans about operations, what goes on or doesn't, what's good for business in the long run. And this publicity today—big deal. What the company needs is a catchy lyric on the radio, and a mascot—we need a mascot kids would call by name."

What popped out of my head was pretty goofy. I said, "How about Ding Dong Dog?" He choked when he heard that, and then he started coughing and he spit out the root-beer barrel onto the floor, his face turning red, and I moved closer and slapped him on the back until he raised his left hand like he was okay, but he wasn't, not completely, and he said, just barely, "Stay here," and that started another fit of coughing, and he left to go into the emergency room for help. I was no doctor, but even I knew all he needed was a watercooler. He was just scared of choking, is all.

I wanted to impress him by making good sales before he got back, so I opened the service door. The cameraman was right there, but he wasn't focused on me. He seemed to be zooming in on something else, something behind me, and I stepped outside to see what that was. There, on top of the hill behind the hospital, right in front of the rectory, the sisters (I counted ten of them) were sitting on chairs in the sun, sitting absolutely still in a straight dark line against the sky, their hands folded. I folded mine too, surreptitiously, my back to all the goings-on, and I prayed hard, right along with them for a few minutes, that the pledges were pouring in. Perhaps there *was* such a thing as charity, when it came right down to saving the lives of little kids. I hoped so, and later on, after I'd eaten two hot pretzels and sauerkraut I bought for lunch at one of the stands, I told Leo that I had to go to the men's room. "So go to the men's room," he said, which I did, but I also beelined it to the hospital lobby to make a donation in my name for twenty-five dollars, for which I was thanked a lot and blessed. I didn't tell Leo anything when I returned, and I didn't let on that I was anxious to tally our sales. I knew we were doing well, even with all our prices cut in half.

At the end of the day, after we'd pulled out and were heading toward Springfield by a back way, through some countryside, Leo said, "Respectable—nothing great, but we'll take it."

I thought he meant that we'd keep our usual commission percentage, which made a kind of sense, though the wrong kind. I assumed all along that I'd be working this last Ding Dong day for free, a sort of payoff to Leo for having picked me up at the police station, and for much more than that, but now that I thought about it, I couldn't imagine Leo settling for zilch, giving up a day's pay for any cause. So I asked him about it. He said, right out, "Relax—nobody's getting gypped but you." Whatever he meant by that, he didn't say, and I let it go.

We crossed a bridge right about where two small streams joined. The water was clear, and the stream widened out beyond the confluence. "Brook trout water," I said, and Leo, glancing quickly down, said, "I guess." Just those two words, throwaways. Maybe he didn't mean to, but when he said that he shoved us eons apart, which didn't matter permanently because I liked him, and didn't, and then liked him again. Leo Tomashek, the science teacher who must have taught his students how opposites attract and collide, and that the universe was formed four and a half billion years ago through a series of prolonged explosions. Big bangs, little bangs. I wanted none of it during our last half hour together. I'd go with harmony, so I steered the conversation away from fish, back to the world we both knew. I asked him who had taken his route for the day, and he told me Lemcool had, for keeps, because yours truly, Leo A. Tomashek, was moving upstairs, and what did I think about "them apples"? Salary, medical benefits, the whole nine yards.

He kept talking in his glory, but I didn't listen anymore. I thought instead about how things changed and didn't, erupted, then quieted down. And I visualized again the tobacco fields and all those migrant pickers I'd seen my first day coming down the rows, and the rows so tall now that only the colored bandannas on their heads would show. I wondered if Lemcool spoke any Spanish, and if not, if he'd bother to learn, possibly take a night class at the community college. And whether or not that one woman still came around each day with the exact change for her two Dixie Cups, and if Lemcool would make lousy jokes about her the way he did about Lynette, whom I would never see again, though I wanted to badly and didn't even know why. To confess, maybe, face-to-face, that I was only eighteen and that the MGB wasn't mine. Sometimes, with the right person, you could break the ice that way, by confessing, then leap toward important things coming right at you out of the blue, powerful things, so that you felt you'd spun away, at least for a little while, from the constant gravity pull of sadness. Not that what was talked about wasn't sad. It was. But you'd feel closer to understanding incidents that half frightened you to death at the time. Like when my father one winter (it was snowing hard) tied up an old volleyball net inside the barn and made me set for him over and over, only a single spotlight on, while he spiked the ball right into the wall only three feet away, spiked it as hard as he could, shouting the names of people who'd let him down. His own father, for one. Stuff like that, crazy stuff you thought you'd buried.

"Buzz Whorley," Leo said, "takes Lemcool's job, and Stapleton takes his, and Charlie Protz gets Stapleton's if he wants to make the switch," and he rattled off the names of every driver until he came to me and then he didn't say anything, like I didn't have a name. But I'd already figured out that I would have moved to Springdale, where there was a playground and a wading pool and some tract houses where the families of servicemen stationed at Westover Air Force Base lived. "A million rug rats," Ronnie Sullivan would inevitably say. "Those pilots, breaking the sound barrier like that, they must develop some kind of wicked sex drive," and he'd snap his long, bony fingers above his head like a matador and pirouette completely around on the ball of one foot. He was moving up the Ding Dong ladder too.

"That's a real pisser," Leo said. I'd had teachers who, minutes before the class would end, expected you to parrot back what you'd learned from them that hour. I didn't intend to do that, get trapped into acknowledging as truth the lessons Leo had taught me. But I didn't want the lecture repeated either, so I stayed neutral. I said, "Yeah."

"Yeah, what?" he said.

"Yeah, nothing. It's a pisser, okay? Come on, Leo, I don't know."

He surprised me. He said, "Neither do I," and he didn't drill me this time with harsh facts designed to unravel the snarl of emotions I felt. He let it go and began staring into the sideview mirrors, mostly into mine, as though someone in a car behind us kept flashing the headlights on and off at us. People did that sometimes, if they wanted ice cream badly enough, pulling you over as if they were cops. And that's what stuck in my head—the cops—so I leaned forward when Leo stopped on the shoulder, and I stared into the mirror.

Nothing there but my own face. And when I turned back, Leo had his hand out. I reached over and shook it, and Leo nodded, nodded with a tight jaw like he wanted badly for me to be all right. He didn't say that or anything else until we got to the bus depot. Then he said, "You traveling like that?" meaning in my Ding Dong whites, and I told him I was. "Good," he said. "Good, good, good," and he rang that bell a bunch of times, but he didn't wait for the few customers who came out of the terminal, who stared at me, and then back at the truck, picking up speed, as though it were driving away alone.

ELEVEN

My father was asleep on the couch when I got home. The TV was going, the sound very low, and Art Linkletter was in the middle of that segment "Kids Say the Darndest Things." I watched it, the way you do coming in on a show, for only a few seconds, and when I looked back at my father his eyes were open, but he didn't move. He said, "Turn it up if you want," and I walked slowly over to the set and clicked it off instead, which seemed like a mistake at first, because he sat up and we faced each other with nothing to say. I had assumed, being gone most of the summer, that we could have talked for days, nonstop, but it was just the opposite.

I gazed over at the blank TV screen, where I imagined Art Linkletter prompting some sullen, stubborn little kid into conversation. He was the master at that, transforming even the camera-shy, stage-frightened voices into song. He'd strike the right chord every time. Only once did I see him really struggle against silence, and that was when a seven-year-old had clammed up tight as a drum, refusing to even shake his head yes or no. I could tell he was furious about something, and no amount of jokes or pleas or deals would change that. Maybe Art Linkletter should have moved on, down the row of easy smiling faces, but he didn't, and still playing to the live audience, he said, "Anything, Billy—you can say anything you want." Billy looked up surprised at this famous adult who nodded yes, go ahead, and he did, without hesitation, leaning forward and staring wild-eyed into the camera lens. He shouted, "This is for you, Kevin, and I really mean it," and he flipped all America the bird. A classic, and I asked my father if he remembered that, which I knew he did, and he stood up and said, "I'm so glad you're back."

"Me too," I said, and it was no longer a lie, and that was good enough for openers.

I wished I had brought him a gift, a box of saltwater taffy, but I hadn't gotten close to the ocean. All I had was money, and I offered to start paying rent, especially since I had decided against college, at least for first semester, but he ignored me, saying, "Steaks for dinner tonight." No arrangements, no big changes. It was time to celebrate, not with Delmonico's, no choice center cuts, but that was fine. We'd see if I had finally acquired a taste for a little gristle, meat you had to fight with awhile. "Chew it well," my father used to say to me. He'd cut my steak into tiny pieces with his Buck knife, which he kept razor sharp, and he'd drop the pieces onto the metal tray of my high chair, and he'd say, "Chew it well." I was too young then to use a fork. Sometimes he'd use his fingers too, which he knew I liked, because he'd spread them, greasy and wide apart when he was finished eating, and he'd get all hunched over and half circle the table, one way, then around to the other side, coming after me like a monster.

Which some people said he was, but they weren't very smart, and it's a good thing the court didn't try to take me away from him. I was all he had and I knew now that he'd raised me pretty well and I intended to remember that. I'd wait for the right time to tell him so. No highfalutin drama about prodigal sons, no announcing my return as advent of a new understanding between us. I'd say instead, "Crack me a beer, would you?" if he was closest to the Styrofoam cooler in the boat some evening, the small aluminum boat I noticed in the backyard when I first arrived. I was already edging the conversation that way when I said, "You're fishing again."

"I will be shortly," he said. "On that you can bet your life." And I would have, on whatever he had said at that moment, and he knew it, and he took a deep breath and squeezed my shoulder as he passed to go downstairs to turn on the sprinkler, and to extend the courtesy of distance while those few words settled. I tried to say them like he had, "On that you can bet your life," but they sounded different on my tongue, something much closer to "Forgive me, please, for the damage I've done."

Next day he covered all the particulars, how he'd gotten the boat and motor and trailer for a song from a guy at the Fisk who'd lost big in a poker game and needed the cash "right now!" The trailer was oversized, originally for a bigger, heavier boat, and it needed to be painted and rewired because neither taillight worked, but it fit the hitch on the station wagon, and the tires were like new, nothing out of line. And I noticed that the trailer was registered—a legal sticker on the license plate, good until December of the following year. No more throwing mud over the tags, a stunt my father tried some years back. But the law kept on him then and they pinched him the very first time he drove into town, to take me to the dentist. I remember how that deputy, his light on but no siren, slid up alongside our car and pointed for my father to pull over, which he did, saying nothing. I could see out the rear window that the deputy was scraping our license plate with his boot toe. Then he got back in his cruiser and made us wait. I knew we'd be late for my appointment. I tried to tell my father that, but he did not want me talking and shook his head no. The deputy finally walked over, holding his pad. He lowered his smug face a little and looked past my father at me and, first thing, started shaking his head, as if to say, "You poor little bastard, seeing all this," but my father stared him down, and the deputy stepped away a bit. He tried to act calm and tough, but he wasn't, always peeking up while he wrote out the ticket. My father didn't rip it up, not right then. He dropped it on the seat between us, and we continued on, and that was that.

Except for the fine that followed, which the court said he could pay through the mail. He never responded, and they revoked his driver's license for two weeks. But as I said, they were tightening the screws on him in those days, trying to tame him down. He never forgave any of them, but that was long over, all done. He'd paid all his bills and had even managed to put a little money away for me for college and now he'd bought himself a fishing rig, and I was hearing all about it, every detail. Like how the motor was a three-horse-power Johnson, the old style with the gas tank on top, but that it was cherry, my father told me, except for the starter cord, which needed a new return spring. Then he had me feel, between my finger and thumb, how he'd feathered out one blade of the prop with a flat file, then with steel wool, getting rid of the gouges.

It meant a lot to me that my father had projects again, and that carpet still needed to be cut and fitted to the floor of the boat, carpet you could take out easily and hose clean.

This wasn't cosmetic—it kept the noise down: no metal on metal if a pair of needlenose pliers got dropped, or even a bell sinker if you were still-fishing shallow on a calm surface. Sound traveled a long way underwater. And the boat needed rod holders for when we trolled slowly for browns and walleyes. He'd get to that too, all in good time, and to building a raised plywood platform up front for storage: life preservers and rain gear and marker buoys, and for the toolbox—you never motored away from shore without a spark-plug wrench and a screwdriver. Space was stingy in a small boat; yet you couldn't afford any clutter either. Eventually it would cost you fish or tackle or worse. Everything—anchor, net, Plano tackle boxes—fit snuggly in its own place.

My father said it was one remedy against chaos, which I guess is why he began tracing again, with a heavy-lead carpenter's pencil, tools that he'd hold up with his left hand against the garage wall, fitting them into a pattern of crazy angles. Then he'd sink a nail at the tool's perfect balance point, and that tool would always hang in that one spot. He hadn't done this since leaving the farm, where each implement hung unused in the final weeks, hung like a collection of leg braces or crutches, reminders of how the bank had crippled him badly, so that he felt too weak to even plant both feet firmly on the base of a shovel or spade, slice it cleanly into the rich earth. But he had recovered some after all these years; he'd Rototilled a long, narrow strip along the side of the backyard, and the tomatoes were ripe, and the green peppers too, and abundant, and he'd planted horseradish, which he pulled up for the first time from the ground for our celebration dinner, and in the kitchen he grated that fat root into fiber, white and delicate, except on the tongue, where even a pinch would clean out your sinuses.

■ ■ ■

I liked watering the garden in the days that followed, un-screwing the sprinkler and attaching instead the heavy nozzle. I'd twist it all the way back for the softest spray, like mist, and I'd watch how the water beaded after a while on the leaves and vegetables and how robins would move closer and closer. It was a crummy trick, but I'd chase those birds away each time one jerked out a worm or a night crawler, and I'd carry it, squirming as though already on a hook, and drop it into the bait box.

But I was missing Phoebe a lot. And after a week at home, watering and reading Balzac and sleeping late, I wrote to her. I didn't want to, not so soon. I recognized the danger of rushing things, that awful custom of flying apart and begging not to be misheard, that you had the words this time to astonish God. Grief did that, transformed you into a healer in your own head, the profit of sorrow. "Recover," that voice whispered, "recover, recover, recover," driving you half-nuts. I didn't want Phoebe to sense any panic, so I began by asking her to send my fishing rod C.O.D. and I talked about the garden and the boat, how we'd landed a hell of a nice batch of smallmouths at Skegemog one evening, all on surface plugs—Hula poppers and jitterbugs—and how we'd prepared the fillets in beer batter late that night. But that all sounded too technical when I reread it, so I crossed it out, and pretty soon I was talking about the full moon I'd watched and how much I wished she and I had been together to see it from the observatory. That was going too far the other way, so I edited that part out too and began again, asking simply if there was any chance, any, of us ever getting back together. I told her I'd wait, giving her all the time she needed, if she could encourage me at all, even a little bit.

She didn't answer. I'd meet the mailman on the front porch, and he'd say each morning, "Sorry, nothing again," and leave an electric bill or a flier for Electrolux or a newspaper of coupons. Once I ran upstairs into the bathroom, locked the door even though my father was gone, and stared, close up, into the dark mirror, repeating, "Sorry, nothing again," faster and faster until it blurred into nonsense, language even Bissell Crouch couldn't have salvaged for his double-talk.

My father said he'd build me a new rod, so I shopped around in the catalogs and settled on a Shakespeare fiberglass blank, nine foot, snake guides and a fighting butt extension so I could go both ways—fly or spin casting. "You pay for the materials," he said. "The labor's on me," and he fastened two small vises to the coffee table in the living room, and for an hour each night before he left for the Fisk, he'd wrap and varnish, and sometimes he'd get down on his knees, and with one eye closed, he'd sight through the tunnel of guides, making sure they were lined up just right. I studied the rod a lot too, in all its stages, and when the glue and varnish were completely dry, he said, "Here," and handed it to me, letting me be the first one to check the action. It had perfect balance and a quick tip and a lot of heft lower down, which I thought he'd like, a pole that could do some real damage. He was death on what he called "finesse anglers," who spooled two-pound test line for the big ones. Effete fishermen—barbless hooks, playing out a single fish for half an hour. "You want to play with it," my father said, "take it home and put it in the bathtub."

When I handed him the new rod, he held it, waist high and out in front of him, and he flipped his wrist up and down, reminding me of a jouster warming up, and he said, "It's no noodle." He said it would take a muskie or a good-size pike to flatten it out, that really it was too much rod for bluegills or crappies or perch, not that I couldn't catch them with it, but that there would be very little fight. I said, "I can still use my ultralight [the one I had left in Massachusetts] for pan fish," and he looked at me like, "And where might it be, by the way?" (a Christmas present from him years back), but he didn't really say anything. I did. I said, "It'll be here." I said it with enough rancor that he raised his eyebrows, then shrugged, like "Okay, okay," and I said, meaning it, "Thanks for the new rod. It's really a beauty, no kidding," but I wanted him to know also that he'd rubbed me the wrong way with that Mr. Insinuation, see-what-I-told-you-about-the-East-Coast look.

That's how on edge I was, and he knew it, so when he found my waders and ultralight on the back stairs (he was just returning from the 11:00 P.M. to 7:00 A.M. shift) he didn't move a thing. He knocked on my bedroom door and peeked his head in and said, "Phoebe's been here." I didn't get dressed. I passed him in the kitchen and said, "Where?" and he pointed outside.

A note was rubber banded to the cork handle, right above the reel, rubber banded like a warranty, I thought, against permanent breakage. Although I was sure she was long gone, I ran barefoot around front and scanned both directions, even though ours was a dead-end street. It was late September, and temperatures had dropped into the low thirties at night, and I felt chilled, but I sat on the curbstone and read Phoebe's note, not a short one, but that's because it was newsy Dear John stuff. It explained, among other things, that "we" had flown in for Bissell's birthday and that Bissell had asked about me a lot, which made Gordon (like I knew the dink) uneasy and very jealous. And that it hadn't helped either that Mr. Crouch, with one of his perfect Malapropisms, a "Bissellism—like father, like son," had said that my father was an inventor of real venison, meaning vision, but remembering also that he hunted deer, though he couldn't dredge up my father's name, referring to him instead as "the good fellow who guzzled sake like H_2O," and didn't I think that was funny?

"Fuck you," I whispered, "and fuck Flash Gordon too and the spaceship you both flew in on, and all the cruddy jokes and small talk, and most of all, fuck this note," which I crumpled up and squeezed and squeezed as though I thought I could fuse each thin, inky letter into one dark blue pulpy bruise. And then I glimpsed my father coming slowly from behind me and I got up yelling "Don't, don't come near me," and when he did, extending one hand slowly, I ran, first to the other side of the street, but I didn't stop there or look back. I picked up speed across the cold, wet front lawns of the neighborhood, and I began hurdling the hedges, my elbows swinging high, and, finally hitting that perfect stride by the end of the long block, I cut diagonally through the busy intersection with the four-way stop. There was a car at each of them. They must have all known I had the right-of-way because they stayed put, and then I could hear them honking behind me, honking at one another, I imagined, for one of them to move, to get the slow rotation started.

I did not resist getting in an hour later when my father got out and opened the passenger door of the station wagon. The heater whined full blast, and the forced hot air stung but felt good after a few minutes on my feet. I wasn't panting anymore either. I had calmed down. To show my father, I buttoned my pajama top. Then I reached for the comb above his visor and I combed my hair straight back. He nodded at me like combing my hair was the sensible thing to do, and he smiled, but I could tell he was frightened, watching me trying to spruce up, like some escaped lunatic he had picked up and was returning to the asylum for good.

T W E L V E

After my crack-up the dailiness of our lives stayed sane. I opened another savings account ("Don't abuse money," my father said, "by letting it sit idle, collecting no interest. You worked hard for it. Now make it work for you!"). Rudimentary economics, but what he said made sense. I'd deposit, risk free, what I could each week from my new job at Huskey Brothers Sunoco. There existed only one Huskey, which wasn't really a hoax, Johnny Huskey explained. "It's sophisticated business strategy," he said, "treating the establishment like it's generations old, an ongoing enterprise." Under that illusion he said he hoped to coast through the days on his laurels.

His passion for carving duck decoys superseded everything else in his life—certainly rebuilding automobile engines, which he reputedly did better than anyone else in town, if you could get him to do it. A bright red poster announcing the regional decoy carving competition was taped to the inside of the station window, this year featuring deep-water ducks: canvasbacks and redheads. Although he had entered a "can," he said he loved redheads best. He said jokingly that he felt conjugal about them. He was the hands-on favorite to win.

"It's not only the contour feathers," he said, "it's the total anatomy. The judges see only the outer layers, sure, but not the artist. He studies even the pinfeathers, the semitransparent shafts, the pink skin around every tiny quill. Then he holds that skin up to the light, as if his eyes were flesh, and he imagines that flesh sticking to bone, and the marrow inside, and he breaks down that matter until he can't imagine anything else, the subject of a larger science than he will ever understand. I'll teach you," he said, "how to carve, but you'll have to ask me a second time, now that you know how I feel, and the kind of love and discipline it takes to do it right." I had asked him casually, as though I might watch him whittle with a jackknife some evening while shooting the breeze on his back porch. A no-no. Johnny Huskey's esthetic blended art and science.

"Whittle?" he said. "You want to whittle? Then get yourself a stick and sharpen the point and impale a marshmallow." He said he knew more about waterfowl than the classroom professors at any university and that maybe someday he'd open a decoy carving school for a select few—before being admitted, they'd have to pass proficiency exams in ornithology, biology, even iconology, though I should always remember, "A duck is a duck is a duck."

Johnny had graduated from Michigan Tech, up in Houghton, where he said he "extracted" a philosophy degree from a university of mining engineers, which had made him odd man out, the odd duck. "Quack, quack," he said.

"Okay," I told him, "I'm asking again. I'd be honored to enroll as your very first student."

"You'll learn more here than you ever will in college—that's a guarantee."

"About carving I will—I know that."

"About *more*, much, much more," Johnny Huskey said,

and the sound of his voice fit his last name as he repeated and emphasized that word, "more, more," sounding a lot like a foghorn.

"**D**ucks will come in like that," he said, "in heavy mist. When it breaks, there they are, sometimes preening but other times floating without movement among the decoys. If you can't tell the live birds from your imitations, even through binoculars, you've passed your final exam. But that's all post-facto. Now you study, my friend, you study."

Johnny won the competition—he reigned as the 1965 decoy king of the northern Lower and entire Upper Peninsula. Jennifer Stubblebean, from Marquette, was crowned queen. Johnny said later that she sure didn't look like a stubblebean. More like a debutante, he said, in her bright Marimekko dress. But carve? Whoa, my God, could she carve. The most beautiful variegated tail feathers he'd ever seen, bar none. And the ear coverts, "auriculars," which he explained improved a bird's hearing, were so finely etched you thought they would riffle in the breeze when you walked past. He'd never heard of her—nobody had.

"Came right out of the woodwork," Johnny said, and he was so enthralled with telling about her that he didn't even pick up on his own pun. Then he told me how collectors and buyers from outdoor galleries statewide, even a few from Wisconsin and Minnesota, pursued her hard—consignment, commission, they didn't care. She told every last one of them that she didn't sell. She said money emptied the soul. Carving for her could never be a business.

"But could it?" I asked Johnny. "I don't mean for her, but for someone else?"

"I sold my winning canvasback for four hundred dollars," Johnny said, and he wasn't just spouting off, your typical loudmouth. He wasn't boasting at all. In fact, I had never heard him so soft-spoken. He said, "I would have traded the money in a second for Jennifer Stubblebean's redhead, and exactly as she did, I would have held it close to my heart and left right away for home." While he talked, he feathered the blade of his jackknife back and forth across a whetstone, then tested the edge against his thumb. I waited for him to go on, but he did not. He went silent instead, having already opened himself up to me enough, maybe too much, the way you do when someone is willing to listen.

Some days I prayed Johnny would dismiss class, but he was anxious to complete phase one—indoctrination. He'd deliver one aphorism after the next, following me out to the gas pumps or standing over me while I changed a car's oil and filter from down in the pit. Often there seemed no sequence to his lectures. He would launch into sexual rituals, then leap to the contents inside the gizzards of wood ducks—acorns, beechnuts, snails, kernels of corn. He described once, in detail, the rape chase of late courtship, explaining how the female, finally choosing her mate, flies into the air to kiss the drake with an open beak. French duck kissing, I thought, but I knew better than to interrupt with a joke. Then he discussed the difference between eclipse and nuptial plumage and told me that the largest number of contour feathers ever counted on one bird was 25,216—a whistling swan killed in 1937, right here in Michigan. He always appeared awestruck after an oddball ditty like that, and then he'd preach: "First you pluck fifteen different species of ducks, sketching each, and the one you come to know best, you discard, and

choose randomly one from the other fourteen, and you observe that species only, all year if there's open water, taking
notes on how the feathers change color in certain light, how
the recurved tail coverts mature during flights." He'd elaborate on feet, although he said they were not part of the
"seen" decoy, and on the eyes and wings and how only after
"comprehending" all the separate parts should I be given my
first block of wood. "You have to draw," he said. "You have
to draw and sketch and take notes."

"What we need is a field trip," I said one morning after
browsing through a book of mallard drawings by Audubon.
Johnny had gotten the book through interlibrary loan, all the
way from Trinity College in Hartford, Connecticut. He'd
also taken out magazine subscriptions for me to *The Living
Bird* and *Waterfowl World*.

"A field trip?" Johnny said.

"Like in hunting," I said.

It was November and snowing and raining, and Johnny
said, in a voice much less scholarly, much less demanding,
"Bingo."

Johnny's Chesapeake could hardly contain herself in the back
of the wrecker, bounding from one side to the other. The
wrecker lights on the roll bar cast a glow, and I watched the
dog through the rear window. The truck bed was slick from
the rain, though it had let up—off, on, off, on—one of those
sloppy, frigid mornings when the cold goes right to your
bones. Whenever the dog lifted her front paws on top of the
heavy canvas mail sacks of decoys, I was sure her first retrieve
of the season would be onto the river of pavement, its dark
current flowing by at sixty miles per hour.

"She's fine," Johnny said. "Relax. Have another cup of

coffee." The Stanley thermos was between us on the seat, on top of our gloves.

"She's gonna jump," I said. "No kidding, Johnny, she's halfway out of the truck right now."

"Then let's get her back in," he said, and he swerved hard, first to the left into the other lane, and then to the right, the wide tires spitting up dirt and gravel from the soft shoulder. Both shotguns, in their cases, slid up against me.

"Jeez, Johnny," I said, and I looked back, and Abigail was still there, soaking wet, her feet spread wide apart, toes splayed, as though she were about to shake, having just swum back and climbed into the blind with another duck.

"She's blockheaded, not suicidal," Johnny said. "She's waited for this morning all year, and she's not going to go kill herself now, do you suppose? I wouldn't stand for it, not from the woman I love."

I told Johnny that my father always had beagles on the farm, rabbit hounds, and that I hadn't been around retrievers much. "That's obvious," he said. "Number one, they're all loco, not only the Chesapeakes, the Labs and goldens too. Sometimes I think they evolved from ducks. Remind me to show you Abigail's webbed feet," and he spent the next several minutes explaining how each stiff hair was actually hollow so that the water beaded off without ever reaching the skin. "You got it," he said, "like feathers." He said, "And retrievers have two flaps inside their noses, one for each nostril, like plugs. A good trainer, a real good one, can teach his dog to dive and swim underwater."

"Aqua hounds, right? Trout retrievers? Come off it."

"That's no lie," Johnny said. "Those wounded ducks, the cripples, will dive and tangle themselves in the rushes, drown themselves rather than get caught, or sometimes they'll hide

under lily pads, only their bills out of the water. For water-fowl, you need a water dog."

Johnny slowed and turned off onto a dirt road, and after another couple of miles, to a two-track where he got out and locked the hubs and took a pee. Ahead, in the high beams, I could see NO TRESPASSING signs tacked to the trunks of the trees.

"I put them there," he said, sliding back into the truck and shifting into four-wheel.

"That takes nerve."

"Not really," Johnny said. "I own this land, seventy-five acres of it."

It was swampy and got worse, but Johnny knew right were to goose the engine, fishtailing through mud and straightening out and sliding sideways again until we hit the high ground, where he killed the lights and we stopped for good. Abigail was out now, on my side, and I aimed my flashlight on her chest so as not to blind her, and I could see her tense and shivering, but Johnny was in no hurry. He sat there, kind of slouched, clinked open his Zippo to light a cigarette, and cracked his window a couple of inches.

"All mine," he said. "All this, and I owe no one a dime." But it was still too dark for me to see what "all this" was. I pointed the flashlight beyond Abigail, but even with the new batteries the beam was swallowed by the thick undergrowth.

"In less than an hour you'll see it," Johnny said, "a first-class aviary. A bird sanctuary, designated such by our own DNR of Michigan. A waterfowl breeding ground. A regular stop on the Canada flyway. Take your pick."

"Any one is worth a lot," I said.

"Amen," he said. "That's exactly what I told the bank. I drove two of those wing-tipped clowns out here to show them what I'd found. Neither brought boots, so they were not interested in taking two steps away from their Wagoneer, that fake wood veneer on the sides. And they both pipe up, a regular Greek chorus, 'Unbuildable without a hell of a lot of fill.' 'Fill, my ass,' I told them when we got back to Michigan National, and when they wouldn't approve my loan request, I reached into my pocket and fanned out, like a gigantic royal flush, ten one-thousand-dollar bills. Then I said, the seller standing right there, 'Unless one of you high rollers intends to raise the stakes, I believe I'm holding the asking price.' I signed the papers, canceled my checking account and the station's account, and tipped my red Peterbilt cap and walked out."

"My father felt that way about his land, farmland," I said, "but he couldn't pay and he lost it."

"I know your father," Johnny said. "I like him. He never took grief from anyone. He used to stop by the station to buy gas, sometimes a buck's worth, always the one ninety, even though I told him it's what's making the engine knock."

"Now I fill up the station wagon once a week for him on the discount," I said.

"He'll never buy his land back on what you save him doing that," Johnny said, just kidding around, but I said, kind of surly, "He doesn't want it back. He's got a garden now, and a boat."

"That's not enough," Johnny said. "What I mean is, that it's not enough for me."

"Not yet it isn't," I said, and Johnny, inhaling deeply so that the tip of his cigarette glowed a few long seconds, answered, "Not ever," and blew the blue smoke slowly against the windshield, fogging it up, and we both listened then to the rain falling again. Johnny was thirty-two years old, and

I don't know what he was thinking, and I didn't ask. Me, I imagined the first flock of mallards descending on the decoys, and how that point duck was a drake, its iridescent green head shining in the first light, and me leading him the way my father had taught me, doggedly, before I could hardly even steady a shotgun, before he got older and quiet and settled for those other things.

I carried the two shotguns, Johnny's Browning automatic and my Remington pump, and Johnny carried the sacks of decoys, one sack over each shoulder. Abigail ran ahead, stopping a lot, staring back. "Just follow her," Johnny said. "She'll lead you right to the blind." He circled wide, and the next time I saw him he was in a camouflaged canoe, fifteen, maybe twenty yards out in front of me, laying out decoys. The bottom was all marl. "You step in there," he had said earlier, while we both strapped on our hip boots, "and they'll find you in hell."

The temperature had dropped, as it always does a few degrees at that time of year, just before daylight. And overhead the clouds were breaking up and moving east. I liked being out here and watching Johnny work alone from the canoe. And I liked having him as my friend, the auto mechanic who rarely talked about that as a skill, which it was, and I was learning it fast, though he hadn't yet given me a single raise.

It wasn't because he was cheap. Labor for money wasn't important to Johnny the way it was to Leo Tomashek, or, in a different way, to my father. That didn't mean Johnny didn't put in the hours—he did. And he never bitched about look where his college degree had gotten him—rebuilding carburetors, adjusting timing chains. He worked and he took days off. He hadn't hunted on the opener like a lot of guys who probably called in sick or put in ahead for a vacation day. But now that the flocks were migrating down, he'd closed up shop. He had a sense of humor about it too, hanging a sign on the station door, a wood sign he carved in about ten minutes. The letters were so symmetrical you'd swear he'd done it with a rotor. The sign said FEELING DISTRACTED—GONE HUNTING.

Johnny said one of the beauties of living in northern Michigan was that you could tell the truth and not have to endure too much bitching. He said he was never leaving. But I thought he might be, permanently, if he didn't sit down in the canoe. I almost yelled that to him, but instead I watched what he was watching, how the pink half-light rippled on the water, and how the raft of decoys moved, slow quarter turns against the anchor line, and how the cattails on the far side of the marsh were just now visible in black.

Abigail sat alert, ears up, beside me in the blind. I touched her head, then the back of her neck, but she didn't move. She never once took her eyes off Johnny. "Good trainers," he had said. He was one, having taught Abigail to stay and heel and to follow a whole series of hand signs, but the way she loved him had little to do with the instinct of the breed to obey commands. I wondered if she had or ever would have a litter of puppies; if so, I wanted one. Two, three weeks' pay—it didn't matter. I'd bring the subject up later. Right now Johnny was paddling in, and Abigail, seeing him close, wagged her tail and licked my hand again and again in anticipation of what was about to begin.

It happened fast. Johnny saw them first, at the level of the trees, but he didn't make a move and neither did I, except to take off my other glove. Down on our knees, heads bent forward, we listened to the sound their wings made, and to their bodies planing in against the water. I hoped we weren't going to open fire on them like that, not sitters. I looked over at Johnny, and he pulled back his sleeve with his teeth and tilted his watch toward me, and then he mouthed, "One minute. One." Seven-fifteen was the legal shooting time.

I didn't think they'd stay. I thought that Abigail would move or that the mallards, confused and quacking, would swim out of range, toward the mist rising at the river mouth, and be gone. But when Johnny eased off his safety, I did too, and even when we stood into clear view, they didn't fly, not immediately, not until we sighted down those long barrels, and then the whole flock was up, and I knew, with my modified choke and magnum loads, that I could have taken out two or three birds with one shot. A single duck veered off left, and I swung with him and fired, and he dropped, and Johnny fired—*ka-bam, ka-bam, ka-bam*—and I could see two more go down, farther out, by a tiny island. I didn't bother taking aim at the three that turned and circled high and kept on going.

"Old Natty Bumppo over here. The Leatherstocking himself," Johnny said. "One shot, one bird," and he ejected his third spent shell, and I watched the smoke rise out of the chamber and I felt good.

"Two for you?" I asked, and Johnny nodded toward Abigail, who was already swimming back with both of them in her soft mouth.

Johnny knelt and took the pair, a hen and a drake, lifting them into the blind by their long necks, the way I'd seen my father carry ducks and geese and grouse. He'd even pose with them hanging like that for an occasional snapshot, as though they couldn't be held any other way—a fish by its gills, a squirrel by its tail, birds by their bony necks. But they could be held less brutally, and Johnny knew how. He let the drake lie on the plywood floor, and using two hands, one opened wide under the breast, the other on top, he stood, pressing the hen close to his hunting jacket as he might a homing pigeon he meant to release soon into the air.

But this one was flying nowhere. A bloody phlegm blistered on the edge of its beak, and the head drooped, seeming so heavy, and when I lifted it I could see where a single lead pellet had entered right below its closed left eye. Johnny thumbed it open to show me the brown iris. And he slowly rotated the duck, sideways, then back, then all the way around, saying, and I think he was quoting from a textbook, note this and note that, "The vermiculated brown-and-white flanks, the buff underpants, the scapulars streaked with black subterminally, the almost red feet." But I remember best what Johnny said after he paused, after he finished his lecture. He said, "Beautiful. Beautiful flight mallards, mature birds," and I simply nodded because I understood that terminology.

I opened the burlap bag, and Johnny lowered the hen carefully in, and then the drake, and Abigail, knee-deep in brackish water, was back with the third, which was floating, head submerged, in front of her chest. "Good girl," Johnny said. "Good Abigail," and he patted her hard on her wide head and scooped up the duck I had killed.

"This one's banded," he said, and without even glancing up at me, he took out his jackknife. He hadn't field-dressed the other two, so I thought he might cut the duck's leg right off at the first joint so I could observe, close up, how the thick skin resembled scales. But he was dissecting nothing. He simply pried open the band and handed it to me and said, "I always hate reading where they're from. It's a little like taking the collar off a dead dog, if you get what I mean."

"Delta Marsh," I said. "Manitoba, Canada," and that seemed like such a long way away.

Johnny said he had a whole necklace of bands, geese and ducks both, not that he ever wore it, a totem like bear claws or eagle feathers, but he called it a necklace just the same. And he said he had a map—he'd show it to me—spread out on a sheet of cork in his workroom, and there were different colored pins—white headed and yellow headed, green, red—a color for each species of duck, puncturing the places these birds had migrated to or from: Squaw Creek National Wildlife Refuge, Mound City, Missouri. McGinnis Slough, Illinois. Kotzebue Sound, Alaska. He said a whole nest of pins sprouted around Saskatchewan, red pins, I imagined, tiny beads of blood. And I imagined two other pins, blue like sky or water, buoys on Galveston Bay. No, not buoys at all, but a pair of mallards having flown two thousand miles together to nest in the Upper Peninsula. Johnny said he had connected all the pins with thin white threads, each one leading finally to northern Michigan, right to this blind, he said, where he'd cut, with the tip of his X-Acto knife, a hole through the map and through the cork where all the threads disappeared in a tangle.

"Is that to determine how far they've traveled?" I said. "And their routes?"

"I guess," Johnny said, "partly. But really, shit, you don't need maps and thread. Flight patterns are predictable. The birds aren't trying to fool us."

He was sounding less and less the hunter-carver, and more the philosopher he studied to become at Michigan Tech, especially when he said, "Distance is unmeasurable."

I knew he did not mean in miles exactly, but I said, not wanting the morning to go sad, "It depends on how many times they've made the trip."

"Enough times to get dead," Johnny said, and he heard something I didn't, but I looked up and saw our second flock—and this one was much bigger—bank toward us from the far end of the marsh when Johnny blew through his duck call, again and again, different lengths and pitches, and he motioned me to get low and tug on the anchor line, which I did, and the decoys came alive on the flat, calm water, excited and calling their pals down, offering rest and safety before the long haul home.

THIRTEEN

I nodded off on the drive back to the station and I didn't wake until Johnny, with a tiny feather of down, tickled my eyelid, then a second time. I brushed his hand away and said, "Yeah, okay, I'm here," and yawned and stretched, my back arched, and pushed open the wrecker door with one foot, and I sat like that a minute, the cool air drifting in across my face. Johnny, already out, yelled back, "Grab those four under the seat," meaning the hen mallards we'd hidden there, those beyond our daily limit.

I carried them, two ducks in each hand, around to the driver's side and lined them up, all stiff and cold now, on the raised concrete island between the Sunoco pumps. I had scraped and painted the island a glossy white a week before and I could still smell the paint a little, though mostly it was the smell of gasoline that floated up strong after the rain. In the puddles I could see the purple and green film floating, not quite the plumage of wings, not even pretty really, but I liked standing there, the two of us dressed in camo, Johnny still wearing his cartridge belt, a double X stamped black on each red shell, his duck call hanging low around his neck. Johnny Huskey, I thought, the man who had referred to himself one afternoon as a north woods grease monkey with a sheepskin in "pondering." But he said he'd wised up, that for four years he'd read and reread the great thinkers and what he'd learned was that all but a handful were bona fide turdheads, psychos. So I wasn't about to tell him, while dividing up the ducks, that everywhere I had ever been or imagined being belonged to this moment and that I wanted it to last. "Come again?" he'd say, and I knew that I'd sound foolish trying to pinpoint, beyond the obvious—shotguns, a trained dog, bloodstains on a glove—what made a person feel so whole, happy and sad and peaceful. So all I said was, "Good trip," and Johnny nodded, both of us tired, and we transferred all the gear into the back of his pickup, and when he lowered the tailgate Abigail jumped up and turned immediately around, and I stepped close, held her by both ears and pressed my nose to hers and sniffed, and then again, and she started licking my face all over, my lips tight, eyes closed.

"This day belongs to the blessed," Johnny said. "Grab a nap. I'll see you tonight at nine o'clock at the Flatiron."

Johnny wanted to meet there late, after the crowd (banshees, he called them) had thinned out. He said, if things fell right, we'd punch in Patsy and Hank and Ernest Tubbs on the free jukebox. Maybe a little "Jambalaya" to fire up, a few rounds of shots and beers, and then, he said, we'd be ready, blurry-eyed, undone by the outline of a single woman and, if she said yes, we'd take turns dancing with her until "the ghosts in our hearts sobbed with sadness." I smiled at that, and he did too, saying that his girlfriend, Eure (pronounced "Your") Storey, would probably be there, and I imagined him introducing her to me: "This, my boy, is Eure Storey."

And maybe it was my story, or at least the beginning of one, and driving home slowly in the wrecker, I wrote a couple of scenes in my head, simple scenes, like how a mysterious woman nobody knew, a woman with jet black hair and blue eyes, Lebanese maybe, would just show up and cross in front of everyone and sit all alone at the end of the long bar and cross her legs, the toe of one shoe pointing upward, her calf muscle stretching tight and hard. We'd stare, all of us would, and finally, turning slowly around on her stool, she'd nod at *me*, the youngest guy there by far, and we'd end up dancing cheek to cheek, saying nothing. And maybe Johnny, who was always on me to start dating, to open up, would shake his head "No, don't do it" to anyone who thought about cutting in. And I know it was a little weird to think this way, but when I fantasized being tipsy on beer and sliding my hand up high on her back, the woman was not a stranger at all, but Lynette Wallaker, overdressed for northern Michigan in her high heels and gray skirt and nylons, but there just the same, thirty-two years old now, smiling and then kissing me on the mouth to end each slow song. I wondered if she'd like it here and if she'd eat a pickled egg and beef jerky and drink Stroh's from a bottle and feel good just sitting in the darkness of a corner table for the time it took to smoke a cigarette (I remembered her brand was Philip Morris) and if she'd invite me again to go home with her. This time I would, not in a white MGB, but in the wrecker, Huskey Brothers painted in red letters on the doors. No hesitations, no high-tailing it back to Phoebe, that dull and predictable action of another story, a true one nobody cared about anymore, a failure.

Even so, I still missed and thought about her a lot, though I knew that was much too sentimental, the kind of sentence that got edited out of a good story. Johnny had said, over a month ago, that for starters I had to let Phoebe go permanently, just forget her, disengage, he said, "let her go. Private day schools, private East Coast college—she's not right for you. Hell," he said, "it's the difference between a goddamn poodle and a coonhound. Come on, wake up, will you?"

He was angry and didn't even look at me the afternoon he said all that—he'd gone into the men's room around the side of the station, left the key in the door and the door wide open, and he rinsed out his coffee mug, a red one with mallards on it, dried the inside with a paper towel, and squeezing it into a pulpy ball, he threw the towel into the plastic wastebasket under the sink. Standing outside in a light rain, almost a mist, I could see his unshaven face, the dark, thick stubble, clearly in the mirror when he stared into it, first at himself, and then, catching my eye behind him, at me. And he said again, but more gently, "Do it—let her go. Believe me, there's no great shortage of good-looking women in this town. Good women too, and all you have to do is mosey on over to the one you like best and say hello."

I was still thinking about that, moseying over, as I parked the wrecker behind my father's station wagon. I knew I'd have to switch the cars, put his in back of the truck so he could get out to go to work. But I kept the engine idling, the heater on low, and I sat there awhile, thinking how Johnny was probably right, not about me finding another girlfriend, but about how a person needed to keep whacking away at the world whenever it turned nasty, and not to knuckle under to it, certainly not to any one woman's "perfidious" handiwork. Occasionally he'd use a hundred-dollar word like that, as he said, to let me know he wasn't completely dead in the brain pan. But that wasn't the language that mattered to me anymore. I liked much better the straight man-talk in the cab of a truck before daylight, or the chatter around the gas pumps or in the service bays. And, still sitting in the wrecker in the driveway, I imagined the words Lynette might whisper, dancing with me at the Flatiron, at any bar, or the words of that "other woman" Johnny assured me I'd meet and like, if not tonight, then sometime soon. If so, maybe I'd promise to cook her a duck dinner, roast wild duck with sausage stuffing, or Chinese duck, something exotic enough to complement the excitement I knew I'd feel, asking, for the second time in my life, for a first date.

I had already begun plucking the birds and sketching and jotting down notes about the color and texture of the outer body feathers by the time my father came downstairs. He stood right behind me, and from my knees in the grass, I glanced back at him, and against the sky I could see how much his hair had thinned in the past few years.

I figured he'd ho-hum it about the hunting, knowing that going out with Johnny was almost a guarantee on ducks. But instead he seemed really excited, patting me a bunch of times on the shoulder, then squeezing the back of my neck as I knelt there wrenching out the sticky entrails, saving the hearts and gizzards. That felt good, his touching me, and I said that the two of us ought to get out for a shoot ourselves. What the hell, if not over decoys, then to slow-walk the river to jump wood ducks.

"Might do," he said, "might do that." But I knew he never would, knew it for certain when he said a few minutes later that he felt kind of chilly and crossed his arms tightly across his chest and climbed slowly back upstairs to watch me awhile longer from the pantry window, a window that darkened when a rain cloud passed directly overhead, his face appearing so white and angular behind the pane, like someone who had spent way too much of his life indoors. No amount of camouflage could disguise the pallor.

And here it was Saturday, and he'd be off soon to the Fisk to punch in for the 3:00 P.M. to 11:00 P.M. shift for eight more hours of overtime at the factory. I guess he felt he still owed me the price of a college education, though I had told him over and over lately that I wasn't going, not for at least a year or two, if ever, and that he should cut back his hours and relax, that the money thing was old hat, unimportant to me. And besides, he *had* saved some money—not a lot, but some. Unlike me, he'd gotten a couple of decent raises, and Johnny had done a major overhaul on the station wagon's engine, charging my father only for parts, and the rent had not been raised in over two years and wouldn't be, and Hazel kept showering him with gifts, even her dead husband's clothes, which my father began to wear around the house— baggy pants and white button-down oxford shirts so that he resembled a professor, which Manny had been before he died, having taught literature for twenty years, my father told me, somewhere downstate.

Once, on the phone, I asked Hazel where, but she answered elliptically, nervously. She said, "There was no prestige in teaching then, not there. They were *un*teachable," she said. "All of them were scared, every one." Then she hung up and didn't call back for several days. When she did, I answered, and she asked for Manny, and, realizing immediately her mistake, she placed the receiver down so silently that I thought the line had suddenly gone dead. A life gone dead, I thought, or gone crazy.

My father had penciled Hazel's number on the wall by the phone. I dialed right back, but she didn't answer. Had she, I don't know what I would have said—maybe that it was okay to mix things up, that the world rocked out of kilter now and then for almost everyone. Something like that, which I believed absolutely and, more recently, didn't at all. Didn't because I felt so good, as though I'd finally been given the go-ahead to be happy, to hunt ducks and to drink at night in bars with a buddy who'd back me, no matter what, and to forget Phoebe Crouch and Amherst College and mostly just to think less, as Johnny had lectured repeatedly, about the inexactness beyond the particulars of each day. Keep it simple. Think things, I told myself. Other women and the auburn color of whiskey in a shot glass held up to the light. And think nothing more about why my father's hair had thinned, why his boat had been turned upside down on two sawhorses so early in the season, the motor winterized and stored in the rear of the garage, buried under a canvas tarp. Think, instead, I told myself again, of late fall and flights of ducks and how cold two hands could feel under the outdoor faucet on the side of the house, the sun back out from behind the clouds, and the clouds devising shapes without names and passing. Think, a nap. Sound sleep.

Which was exactly what I had, five hours of it, so I felt rested, ready and excited about the prospects for the night, about driving the wrecker to the Flatiron by myself, like maybe I was the owner of a station. In the shower, the hot spray of the nozzle massaging my neck and back, I sang, over and over, the chorus to "Do Wah Diddy Diddy," and then that ballad by Jimmy Dean I'd always liked—"Big Bad John," about the fabled miner who, with one punch, "sent a Louisiana fellow to the promised land."

I seriously doubted that Big John ever splashed on any cologne, but I did, some Canoe, right after drying off and toweling a clear oval in the steamy mirror. Good features, I thought, and a clear complexion and my hair had grown a good ways over my ears, which my father wasn't crazy about (he called it Beatle hair), but I liked it that way and I sensed the women would too. I brushed my teeth and put on my faded blue jeans and flexed, trying to expand my chest, like Big John must have, holding up that last main timber just long enough for those other miners to scramble up, scramble to safety. Big muscles I didn't have—I'd be lucky if I could carry a woman across the dance floor without straining, but I wanted to try. Tonight I could be anyone I wanted, and leaning close to the mirror, I experimented with different faces: the confident, the belligerent, the pouty even (in case of a brush-off), the bemused. And then I smiled and whispered, "You sly dog," and then I barked, I growled.

"**J**oyce Tobias," Johnny said, "but don't even think about it. She's got more problems than Carter's got liver pills. Plus she's married."

I had just asked him about our waitress, not that I had designs on her. I didn't. I was just talking and acting big, though I did like the way she said, "Gentlemen?" and slid a paper coaster that said, in red and blue letters, Flatiron, in front of each of us. Johnny was right as usual—she didn't card me, and later, about ten-thirty, when she brought over a third round of beers, she gave them to us free, squeezing my hand shut on the dollar bill I held out to her, saying, "This one's on the house." Johnny, whose back was to the bar, turned partway around and nodded to the bartender and raised his mug, and I did too, and I sipped through the foam when Johnny sipped, then wiped my lips with the back of my hand. Not everyone in the bar knew him, but a lot of people did, including the other waitress, who, when we'd first walked in, put down a full tray of drinks on an empty table, and on her tiptoes hugged Johnny around the neck, then kissed him on both cheeks, and asked where he'd been. "Where," she said, and punched him softly in the middle of his chest. The perfect entry, I thought, all eyes on us as we headed toward the back of the room, past the stuffed animal heads on the walls above the booths—moose, elk, buffalo, black bear, Michigan whitetail, their glass eyes dulled from staring for years through all that smoke. They were lousy mounts—old, tattered, dusty even.

Johnny lit up first thing after sitting down, took a deep drag from his cigarette, and before exhaling, leaned back in his chair, scanned the barroom, and said to me, "We're early."

But we weren't early. Eure Storey never showed, and the TV stayed on while the jukebox played over it and nobody danced, which was fine by me. Johnny seemed antsy, though, and downing beers much faster than me, he said, "Order me another one, and a shot of Wild Turkey. I've got to go take a whizz." I could see, from my angle in the bar mirror, partway down the hall to the rest rooms. There was a pay phone on the wall, and Johnny stopped there, dropped in a dime, and dialed. I couldn't see his face, his lips, but when he hung up he slid the dime from the coin return with one finger into his palm. No answer. He redialed, and then a third time, easing the receiver away from his ear once, listening, I guessed, to the faint rings, then hanging up again and lighting another cigarette. I hoped he wasn't calling women on my account, now that he was more than a little drunk, deciding to force the night. We'd come back another time, I thought, get luckier. Or try another bar next time, no big deal.

I pretended to be watching the news when Johnny returned. "Ah, the death count," he said, motioning with his cigarette toward the screen. "Christ, a new one-week record. This thing's going to mushroom into a real war yet," he said, referring to the 240 marines killed in action in Vietnam. "You need a reason to go to college?" he said. "To get back to the books, the big thinkers? There it is." Then he said, leaning closer to me, "Eight weeks basic at Camp Le Jeune or Fort Bragg or some other hellhole in South Carolina or Texas. Then, poof, you're gone, a happy hello to Da Nang."

"Not this kid," I said, and smiled. "No way. I'm a pacifist." I felt light-headed and slurred my words.

"Not the way you shoot ducks you ain't." Johnny would do that, mention places I'd never heard of, or books by Kierkegaard or Nietzsche or Reinhold Niebuhr, some of the same titles I'd seen in Manny's library, and a sentence or two later, full of "ain't"s and "it don't matter"s and preacherlike "by God"s, he'd shift into his redneck dialect.

Johnny, cynical now, said to Joyce, who was collecting from me for the fourth round, "Here's one for General Westmoreland, for the troops," and glaring straight up at her, he belted down the shot of whiskey.

"Sure," Joyce said, "whatever," and put my change on the table and turned away.

"Whatever," Johnny said too. "Whatever the hell in this world. That's the ticket. *Que sera sera.* Whatever will be will be."

By the time we left, Johnny had had a beakful. That other waitress who had kissed him watched us leave, but she said nothing. Nor did the bartender, though he nodded to me when I said thanks on our way out. I was pretty far gone too, but not like Johnny, not stumbling drunk, not two-hands-leaning-on-the-hood-of-the-wrecker drunk. He kept that pose, stiff-armed, his head down, and he said, "Shit, Buddy." He said, "Mother of Christ." His pickup was parked about ten yards away.

I thought he was about to get sick, but he didn't and, when I asked him if he was okay, he said, "No, I'm not okay, soldier, but even shit-faced I'm better than you. I'm thirty-three next March," he said. "Double threes," and he looked over at me, his eyes dark slits. "Uncle Sam drafts eighteen-, nineteen-year-olds. Kids," he said. "What do kids know about killing? What do they know?"

He'd been crazy-talking like that, ranting and raving about the war, ever since the late news, first inside the bar and now outside in the cold, the night clear, no wind.

"Come on, Johnny—it's freezing," I said. "It's time to go home."

Lifting one hand away from the hood, almost in slow motion, he saluted me, and losing his balance, he veered sideways but didn't fall. Then he faced me in the dark from a few feet away, and in the headlights of a car leaving the unpaved lot, we must have looked like two guys about to get into it, two friends, drunk, arguing about something idiotic. I figured, in his condition, I could probably hold my own, maybe even sucker-punch him, my best right hook to his chin. Except for a sore jaw in the morning he wouldn't remember the fight ever happened.

"You bum," he said, and he was laughing and pointing at me and wobbling back and forth. "You're the smartest goddamn kid I ever met. Go back to school," he said.

"Christ," and he paused and stared into the sky. I did too, the stars beginning to swirl, so I closed my eyes, pressed my lids tight, stayed still until the spinning stopped. I heard Johnny's pickup start, the door close, saw the lights blink on, first the high beams, then the low. Then the engine stalled, and he started it again, revving it hard this time in neutral. Though I didn't want him driving, I didn't say that when he pulled up next to me, his window rolled down, his elbow sticking out. But I did speak first. I said, "Good-night," and Johnny seemed to watch the shape my breath made rising, tiny ghost shapes.

"Crazy," he said, and he sounded almost sober, "to consider dying at your age."

"So don't," I said jokingly. "It'll keep you awake, ruin your beauty sleep."

"Oh, I'll sleep all right," Johnny said. "Don't worry about me. I'll sleep fine. Remember, I'm almost thirty-three. This war don't need me."

My father was still awake. He wasn't waiting up for me, though—I was pretty sure about that, and sure that he wouldn't give me the third degree even if I did walk in half-crocked. But I didn't want to see him. On the drive home I had stopped at the Bluebill, an all-night diner, for a large coffee to go, and I still had half a cup, which I sipped, hoping the lights would go off upstairs. They didn't, and the wrecker had no radio, and all I kept thinking about was the war turning real: the "death count," the "kill ratio," like an odds game— 180 South Vietnamese dead, 420 Vietcong. I carried a draft card in my wallet—1-A. Choice. Or, as Johnny had said, like prime chuck. Not over coals, he said. Not broiled. Napalmed, medium well. One hundred twenty-five thousand servicemen in Vietnam. The war was turning real. Norman Morrison, a Quaker, had already burned himself to death on the Pentagon steps in protest. Roger Allen LaPorte, a week later, in flames in front of the United Nations. Real facts, real people dying. Hemingway: "In the fall the war was always there, but we did not go to it any more." I wasn't going either. The war had not mattered to me much until now, it being "in another country." And we had no business there; even my father, who decreed almost nothing these days, said so, calling Lyndon Johnson a horse's ass. Perhaps I could enter the seminary or flee to Canada (Johnny said they welcomed draft dodgers) or become a hermit, hiding out so far back in the woods I'd cease to exist. I could keep journals the whole time, I thought, *The Hermit Journals*. Or, as Johnny advised, I could register for second semester classes at U of M. "Play it smart," he said. "Get the degree. It didn't exactly kill me now, did it?"

I thought then about Manny, and about his library, the books I'd read (over a hundred already) from his shelves, those I intended to. And I remembered the titles Mrs. Sullivan had told me were un-American when I was twelve, and how I'd since read and loved all of them. Screwy teachers, cautious, timid, filching so early from their students that wild impulse to disagree, to dissent even before they knew that word, the risks one takes to keep from being brainwashed. Which is what I knew I'd do, resist this war, say no to the Selective Service if they came after me. And no to the FBI. Arrest the real criminals, Mr. Hoover! Begin with our president. And arrest the Congress and the designers of the B-52 and the chemical factories downstate. Arrest Dow. Arrest the warlords, Dean Rusk and Robert McNamara, and sentence those lunatics to life—keep them behind bars. If I had to,

I'd go to jail and never leave my cell—I'd even request solitary. "Give it a rest," Johnny would have said to all this nonsense. "We've got a million martyrs. Buddy, for God's sake, just go back to the books."

I eased the wrecker door closed, took a pee in the grass, then unlocked the back door to Hazel's apartment, keeping all the lights off until I drew the shades tight to the sills in the library. I felt around in the dark, like a blind man, and clicked on Manny's desk lamp. I sat down in his chair, sat forward with my elbows on the green blotter, my head in my hands, and I could hear the muted sounds of bombs exploding on the TV upstairs, the "Late, Late Show," most likely, some patriotic World War II movie, John Wayne or Jeff Chandler. And I imagined that the library was deep underground, a bomb shelter where I could sit out the war and read and read and still not make a dent in the thousands and thousands of volumes surrounding me—collections of poems, novels, history and philosophy books, plays, literary journals. How many had Manny read? And why that single poster, a reproduction of Robert Motherwell's *Elegy to the Spanish Republic*, framed under glass and hanging on the far wall. My father said, when he first saw it, that it looked to him like bull's balls. I liked it, though it did seem kind of bleak, dark, globular. Maybe bull's balls.

I got up, and without turning on any other lights, I found a knife in the kitchen, not sharp, but strong enough to jimmy open Manny's desk drawer. Over the years I had searched for the desk key lots of times, standing on a chair once and sliding my fingers through the thin film of dust above the doorjamb, and feeling, on my knees, under the edges of the rug. Sometimes I imagined the key stuck between the pages of certain books, and I'd open them, hold the covers apart like wings, and shake them, but nothing ever fell out, nothing but a memo one time from a college Dean Somebody-or-Other, saying *"See me immediately!"* The book *Of Mice and Men* was one of my favorites back then (it was the summer we first moved in) when snooping around afternoons seemed innocent enough and fun. And now I'd busted in, broken the lock, and I didn't even know why. Maybe to solve the mystery I had invented about Manny Schwartz, who must have conspired against the world to get away with building a room like this, a refuge, and already he was dead. And I was half-drunk and afraid of dying in Vietnam, and Hazel had gone crazy, my father turning more and more passive, dulled by the slow circuitry of his life.

I pulled open the drawer, half-expecting to find a handgun or a cyanide capsule, something to make a real story of this night. But all I found was a large manila envelope, a quotation from Oscar Wilde typed on the outside: "The books that the world calls immoral are the books that show the world its own shame."

I dumped the contents on the desk, newspaper clippings, lots of them. Manny, in 1954, when I was eight years old and still on the farm, had been fired for refusing to "teach as directed," which meant, one article said, that he changed his booklist. "Seditious," another article called it, mentioning the names of writers—Eugene O'Neill, Lillian Hellman, Richard Wright, D. H. Lawrence, and a man whose work I didn't know, John Dos Passos. I searched the stacks until I found *42nd Parallel*, a signed edition. The inscription did not say "To the cause," or "First Amendment rights," or "Freedom first." It said simply "Good wishes," and I read no farther, closing the book, sliding it back. Upstairs the bombing had stopped. I wondered what time it was in

Vietnam, if the skies were quiet above the villages. And I wondered if Johnny had made it home safely. Then I heard my father coming down the stairs and I switched off the lamp, stood absolutely still in the dark. He used the bathroom, flushed the toilet, left to go back up to bed. He coughed just once before shutting the door, and I started to cry, softly, to myself. One cough, I thought, as if to let me know he was there, still breathing, finishing his day.

F O U R T E E N

"Think about it a minute," I said, but Johnny didn't want to. He said it wasn't a thinking man's world. He said a Christmas truce in Vietnam amounted to a hill of beans.

"Ten days ago we dropped twelve tons of explosives on Haiphong, and you say, maybe, just maybe, in the holiday spirit, we're finally coming to our senses, that we'll see an end to the goddamn war yet. Wishful thinking, but let me clue you in—this war's going to rage and rage a long time before it's over. You mark my words. Remember I said this."

"Pope Paul thinks the truce is a good sign," I said, "and so do I. It sure can't hurt. And I can wish, can't I?"

"Wish in one hand," Johnny said, "and piss in the other. See which one fills up first."

My father, buttering the last dinner roll and glancing up, first at Johnny, and then at me, said, "How about a truce between the two of you? How about we should listen to some carols while I make the coffee. Then I've got to shoot over to Hazel's and drop off a present." It was midafternoon, and we'd been eating and talking for over two hours, and laughing a lot too, at least before the Vietnam argument. Hazel, the day before, had sent us two huge poinsettias from Klump Floral and Gifts. The card said "Merry Xmas, Yrs., Hazel

Schwartz." The clay pots were wrapped with red and silver aluminum foil.

"Sure, why not?" Johnny said. "But one last thing, real fast," and he leaned forward, across the table from me, and he said, staring right at me, "You're way off base on this one, chump. Ho Chi Minh doesn't answer to the Vatican, and figure it out—prayers don't disarm bombs. Use your head. The real secret to surviving this whole business is holding your nose."

Earlier, when we first sat down, my father had said Christmas grace, and I had said aloud, "Amen," and Johnny had too, and I lit a square red candle then, which still burned on the table; and scented with cinnamon, it smelled good, the small flame wavering back and forth a little each time a dish was passed around—baked mallard breasts, asparagus in hollandaise sauce, a spinach casserole kept hot above a tin of Sterno, and a French Canadian dish I had never eaten before, a *tortiere* pie, Johnny's contribution to the dinner. We'd been sipping some Christmas spirits too, Johnny most of all, eggnog and rum, and as he had, half-drunk that night at the Flatiron, he'd gotten kind of loud, toasting, mockingly, the U.S. military brain trust—Lyndon Johnson and Hubert Humphrey and Averell Harriman, whose name I'd heard often on the evening news, but didn't know what it was he did—ambassador of something or other. Johnny knew what they all did, the monsters, as he called them.

Hazel's Victrola (I had lugged it upstairs earlier) was on the floor right behind me, stacked with my father's Christmas albums. I turned partway around in my seat and pressed the start button, and a record dropped onto the turntable. Then the arm slid over, lowered itself, the needle sounding scratchy for a few seconds until Bing Crosby's holiday voice filled the dining room with "Hark, the Herald Angels Sing." We listened to it and to "Silent Night" and to "Oh, Come, All Ye Faithful." Then my father was back from downstairs, and then from our kitchen, carrying a sterling silver serving tray, the polished bottom reflecting the light of the candle. On the tray the electric percolator, cubes of sugar in a silver bowl, a small pitcher of cream—all Hazel's. As was the set of Revere Ware hanging on the hooks above our stove. And the blender we'd used for the eggnog and rum was Hazel's, and the dark wooden salad bowl Johnny was picking from, distracted now, diffident.

My father especially had prepared hard. He wanted more rituals in his life, more tradition. He had baked brownies early that morning in Hazel's oven and he brought those out on a warm plate, having saved and wrapped in paper napkins a few brownies for her. I didn't know if he had invited Hazel over or not. Probably not, though I knew she wasn't Jewish, not by birth anyhow. Her maiden name was Martini (shaken, not stirred, I joked once, but my father, unfamiliar with Agent 007, hadn't thought it funny). She had known Christmas. I knew that because I had carried a box of her ornaments upstairs to decorate our tree—bubblers and plastic icicles, a few strings of blue lights, thin boxes of tinsel. And underneath, on a clean sheet doubled over, I had arranged the manger, her manger (wise men, some camels), then her Star of David, or Manny's star, on the very top of the Douglas fir. I imagined Hazel spending Christmas alone, a few cards—"Season's Greetings"—taped to the doorjamb, the blinds drawn. So I was glad my father was going over to see her, and since our dinner was winding down, I was about to ask to go with him to meet Hazel, which I had never done, not in almost eight years. But the phone rang, and it was

Phoebe calling me from home, and I didn't think about Hazel again for several days.

"Drive me home," Johnny said, "and take the pickup. Really. Bring it by later, or even tomorrow morning—I'm not going anywhere except to bed." And Christmas dinner ended just like that. My father put on his coat and hat and left before we did, shaking hands first with Johnny, wishing him a Happy New Year. I blew out the candle, and Johnny picked up the gift I had given him, a leather collar for Abigail, her name etched on a bronze plaque. And he picked up the decoy I had carved for my father and said, "Not bad. I don't care for the eyes, though." I had seen a color photograph of an albino mallard in an issue of *Wildfowl World*, and I'd given my decoy pinkish white eyes—a freak duck, Johnny called it. Too self-conscious. He said it would give anyone the heebie-jeebies after a while—those "rabbit eyes" staring down from the mantel. But he complimented me on my mechanics, the precision lines of the contour feathers. "Good steady hand," he said, but it was shaking quite a bit a few minutes later when I tried to light a Lucky Strike I bummed from him.

"Here," he said, and he reached under the seat. "Here, take a hit of this." He handed me a pint of Old Museum bourbon. I unscrewed the top and drank. "Wow," I said, "whoa," my stomach burning. "Holy cow, what is this?" the words sounding croupy, rising from way back in my throat. I studied the label. Johnny laughed and slapped me on the shoulder. "Emergency octane," he said. "Fire up—burn rubber."

"What is this stuff?" I asked, grimacing, exaggerating the harsh aftertaste.

"Pure, unadulterated rotgut. The absolute cheapest bar

bourbon ever distilled. Bowery brew," he said. "Give it here," and he reached for the bottle, and before taking a swig, he toasted me. He said, "Here's to perpetuity, things coming back around. Here's to eternal recurrence."

"I don't think so," I said. "Nothing like that. We'll talk awhile, see what's what."

"Where at?" Johnny asked. "You going over to her house?"

"No," I said, though Phoebe had suggested a holiday drink in the observatory for old time's sake. "I'm meeting her in a half hour at the Bluebill." It was the only place I knew for sure was open on Christmas.

"Squirm, squirm," Johnny said, but I was already calming down a bit, relaxing with the booze, and I took another pull off the bottle, and the bourbon went down more smoothly this time.

"Maybe she still has the warm form for you after all," Johnny said, "and maybe she don't. Some of both, I'd guess. You be careful with her, you hear me? Hey, Casanova," he said when I didn't answer, "you hear me?"

"What?" I said. "Yes, I hear you," but I was facing away, out the window into a light, fine snow, not really listening. Wreaths hung from the front doors of most of the houses, and almost no traffic moved through the neighborhood. At the end of the block, attached to the Chillsons' chimney, a lighted plastic Santa—extra fat, extra jolly—smiled down on us as we passed.

"Why'd we create him so goddamn fat?" Johnny said.

I shrugged. I said, "I don't know."

"I do," Johnny said, "because this America *is* fat. It's all Fat City, a country of excess."

I smiled over at him, nodded yes like I agreed, but I liked the idea of kids believing presents arrived by sleigh from the

North Pole if they'd been good all year. No coal in their stockings—just old Saint Nick, gliding lickety-split from rooftop to rooftop in the dark, his sack of presents always bulging over his shoulder.

"It's all that milk and cookies," I said. "You probably left him a snack yourself when you were a kid."

"Sure, I did," Johnny said. "Of course." He slowed for the intersection of Crawford and Davenport. "Of course, but my children, if I ever have any, they'll know the fat man as an American hype. Let us praise him," Johnny said, and he started singing:

> "He's making a list and checking it twice,
> He's going to find out who's naughty and nice,
> Santa Claus is coming to town."

I didn't say so, but I had made a list too, and Phoebe was on it, along with my father and Johnny, but staring through the brightly lighted window of Ashmun Jewelers one shopping night last week, I crossed her name out, just crossed it out, eliminated her. Now I wondered if she had shopped special for me and I wished right then I'd bought her that string of pearls I had looked at at least a half dozen times. Each time I had the cash with me, three hundred dollars, in my pants pocket. But my last time downtown I angled across Main Street to the bookstore instead, where I bought cards for Lynette Wallaker and Mark Elkhart and Leo Tomashek, and one card, a fifty center with a velvet green Christmas tree and velvet red balls on the front, for the whole Crouch family, which is how I addressed it—The Crouch Family. I wrote nothing inside. Only my name. I licked the envelope and then the stamp and dropped the card into the mailbox on the corner outside. I was already sitting in the station wagon when my father got back with his large box of Whitman's Sampler, the deluxe assortment, for Hazel.

"All done already?" he asked, and I said, "Yes," as shoppers passed and passed on the sidewalk, their arms full of packages, making it impossible for them to reach for any loose change in their pockets or purses when they passed the Salvation Army woman ringing her bell, shifting from foot to foot in the cold.

I thought, after Johnny dropped himself off, about doubling back to my house and running back upstairs and rewrapping the book of essays he'd given me, by William James, *The Will To Believe*, a kind of extra present, along with a complete set of new decoy carving tools, the oak handles deep grained. "Never arrive empty-handed," my father had advised years ago, driving me that first night to Phoebe's for dinner. Empty-handed, I thought, empty-handed, and I reached for the bourbon just as Johnny pulled up and stopped in front of his house, but he grabbed my wrist and said, "You'll be an easy target if you're drunk. You want to be loose, not shit-faced. Don't have any more until after you see her." He let go then, said, "Here," and twisted the cap back on and tossed me the bottle. "Keep it for later, when you're alone, or for back here if you want to share a nightcap, if you need to talk." He lowered his head a little and looked beyond me toward his house and said, "Look, up there." I turned, and Abigail's head was wedged between the white curtains in the upstairs window.

"She sleeps on my bed whenever I leave her," Johnny said.

"It's the one thing I couldn't train her not to do." His eyes were closing slightly. "And she waits," he said. "Imagine that, all day."

"We should all be missed that much," I said, and Johnny, knowing that I really meant by other people, not dogs, said, "Who'd be able to stand it? Not me," he said, "and not you either, not anyone I've ever met. We don't deserve to be loved that much."

"I guess," I said, but I believed I could have loved Phoebe like that, completely and forever, had she allowed it. "Wrong," Johnny had said some weeks back, that it was exactly that kind of single-minded devotion that scared women off, but Phoebe had never said that to me. And anyway, what made Johnny Huskey such an expert on affairs of the heart? Nothing, that's what. He drank too much and fell for too many different women. As he admitted, he'd been back to the Flatiron by himself and had scored with that waitress who had kissed him when we first walked in that night. There was something between them—that was obvious—a "sometimes" romance for his "sometimes" girl-friends. Like Eure Storey, a ghost girlfriend. Nothing I wanted. It had to be all or nothing. I told him that as he was getting out of the pickup, and he said, "All or nothing? Good, a man who knows his own mind. A rare quality these days. I like that," Johnny said sarcastically. "Yes, sir, an ultima-tum, the old either/or. You'll get zilch, *nada*, if you offer that option to Phoebe Crouch."

"You don't know that," I said. "What do you know anyway about commitment to a single woman—tell me that. Go on—spit it out."

"I was married once," Johnny said, "though I don't talk about it, not often I don't. I never had any kids, paid no alimony, no nothing. A simple divorce. She gave me my walking papers, and I walked. And that day, my friend, has eclipsed everything else in my life." He was speaking softly, drifting—I could see it in his eyes. A bad subject. "Ten years ago," he said, "ten years. And if she asked me, I'd stumble back to her tomorrow, wherever she is, even though I haven't seen or heard from her in all that time. And you know what? That would be the dumbest thing in the world I could ever do, but I would," he said. "I'd do it, honest to God I would," and he slammed the truck door and started waving Abigail's new Christmas collar back and forth above his head so she could see it, and she left the bedroom window, a one-man dog who'd be waiting by the front door when it opened, waiting for when the only person who ever really mattered to her stepped in.

Only two cars were parked in front of the Bluebill, one of them Mr. Crouch's Continental. I pulled up slowly alongside and looked in. Phoebe was not there. The snow had stopped, and because of the late sun's glare on the glass, I could not see inside the diner. A kind of two-way mirror, I thought, and for a minute I stood in the gravel lot beside the pickup, shading my eyes.

Funny how I felt suddenly guilty and didn't even know what about. Not having contacted Phoebe in months? No present for her? I didn't think so, not really. I didn't know what it was, and it didn't matter, because when I entered she was already standing in the aisle between the worn Formica counter and the booths, and she smiled more and more as I walked toward her, all the way to the back, where, on her tiptoes, she kissed me on the lips and hugged me around the neck and said my name over and over. I remember how the neon dials of the clock behind her on the wall seemed so pink, how the second hand seemed to pause a long time between ticks, the world almost stopping, standing still. I didn't want her to ever let go, and when she started to, I pulled her close again. I pulled her very close and held on tightly, her head sideways so that her cheek lay flat on my chest, my chin on top of her head.

"You've been drinking," Phoebe finally said, looking up at me. "Why don't we go someplace else so I can catch up? Let's get out of here and go up to the observatory." She paused. "I miss what we had," she said. "I miss that a lot now. We can check the sky calendar. Look, it's clear outside now. We'll be able to watch the moon slide past Venus."

I turned to the waitress behind the counter and said, "Another coffee. Please." Phoebe's cup was half-empty. "And a refill here."

I took off my denim jacket and hung it on the aluminum coatrack, right next to Phoebe's new London Fog, the belt folded backward, her long mohair scarf dangling almost to the floor from another hook. I kissed her high on her forehead, half on her hairline, and I said, "Come sit down first," and holding her hand I slid into one side of the booth, Phoebe into the other. I stared at her fingernails, the top half of each one painted white. "A French manicure," she said. "Silly, isn't it?" I said I liked it.

And she wore her hair up, in a way I hadn't seen her do before, except for a few seconds in front of a mirror now and then, always asking me, "What do you think—would you like me to wear it up for you sometimes?" I had always said no, that I liked it down or brushed back into a ponytail. But I did like it up. She looked older, more sophisticated. Smith College sophisticated. An East Coast look, that kind of refinement. And her ears were pierced, a turquoise crescent moon dangling from each lobe. Had we been in the observatory, I know I couldn't have resisted touching the back of her neck with my fingertips, or feeling those loose strands of hair behind her ear, the soft, soft skin there.

"I promise," she began, but I didn't let her finish. I said, "Not yet, Phoebe. Please wait. That's too fast. Tell me about your family. How's Bissell?"

She pulled her hand away, not quickly, and lifted her cup and sipped slowly, staring me in the eyes. Then, reaching into her pocketbook, she lifted out a leather cigarette case, gold trim around the top, and she opened it, slid out a filtered cigarette. "Got a light?" she asked. I had a book of matches in my shirt pocket, the book I had used to light the Christmas candle at dinner. There were three matches left. I ripped one out, closed the cover, flicked the blue head on the emery. "Thanks," she said, leaning back, blowing the smoke off to the side, away from my face.

"Bissell's Bissell," she said. "Destructive. He makes my mother cry. Last week he took a machete to the shrubs, massacred them, in the front and back of the house. My parents are worried sick. I think they'll take him to see someone, if they can get him to go." She paused. "But tell me about you," she said. "How have you been?"

The waitress brought my coffee, a warm-up for Phoebe. I poured what had spilled onto the saucer back into my cup, then some cream, and stirred. How was I? A tough question. Recovering, I thought. Getting by. Good days, bad days, all that *comme ci, comme ça* drivel, as Johnny called it, wishy-washy talk, glib chatter. So I said simply, "Good. I mean, I'm okay a lot of the time. I haven't exactly flourished," I said, "but I've got a job, some money saved," and I talked then nonstop about starting college second semester at U of M, and I mentioned a few books I'd read, to which Phoebe did not respond, and I described my Christmas presents— the carving set from Johnny Huskey, the briefcase from my father, a fountain pen clipped to one of the inside pouches, a white ink eraser, a clear plastic ruler. "School days again," I said, a little embarrassed. Then I said, "And you? Did you get stocks again?" and Phoebe nodded, lifting her eyebrows. "Of course," she said, and laughed. "Always the future— two hundred shares of Dow Chemical this time. Thank you very much, creative grandparents."

"Unload it," I said. "It's poison. Cash it in."

"So you're a stockbroker now," she said, good-humoredly. "I will. I'll sell it at a profit," she said, "in a couple of years, or whoever does that for me will, the lawyers, I guess."

I leapfrogged from that to Gordon. Maybe *I* was moving too fast now, sniping even, but she didn't react. She said, matter-of-factly, "That's over. It has been."

"Still writing his epic?" I asked, attacking. A dangerous maneuver, but I risked it.

"I wouldn't know. If so, he's writing it in Vietnam. He was about to get drafted, so he signed up, enlisted in the marines. He said it was time to see the world, that he'd had it with those dead asses at the hospital, the vets. That's what he called them. He said anything was preferable to that, even killing. I don't know," Phoebe said, "about seeing the world, I mean. There are better ways than that." I agreed. "I'm glad," she said, and she explained that she was going to spend her spring quarter abroad, and she invited me, right out of the blue, to join her in Paris if I could swing it. "We'll travel together overnight on trains," she said. "You always talked about seeing Europe. You did, you know."

"Yes," I said, and I thought, Gay Paree. Sure, just like that, pick up and go, and I could feel the bourbon and I closed my eyes and I imagined sparks flying from the tracks below us as we made love in the sleeper, or just lay on our backs, side by side, staring up into the darkness, the line of cars rattling along those shiny rails.

"You okay?" Phoebe said, reaching over and touching the back of my hand. I opened my eyes and looked outside and watched a car slow down, the first to approach since I arrived, its blinker pulsing. But the driver must have thought better of such a deserted diner on Christmas, and he stepped on the gas, passed on.

"Let's leave," Phoebe said, watching the car disappear out of sight. "I want to get out of here. Really, it's depressing." She was staring at me again, smoking a second cigarette, her face stern, deadpan. I could feel myself smiling, not even sure if it was a happy smile or a cynical grin, and I felt suddenly hot, sweaty, confused, and I said, "Excuse me a minute. I'll be right back." I left for the men's room, wanting to hold that same expression in the mirror, to examine, close up, my own face, simulate my response to Phoebe's loose-tongued invitation to travel with her to France. What a joke, Johnny would have said. "France," and he would have started in: "Ah, *madame, parlez-vous*, a humma humma." She'd invited me so nonchalantly, as though nothing had happened between us, as though we had solved, in less than half an hour in the back booth of an abandoned diner, four solid months of separation, absolute silence.

I locked the bathroom door. I closed my eyes again and leaned forward, my head spinning now, and I knew I was much drunker than I had thought, or plain poisoned from that rotgut of Johnny's. "Shit," I said. "Damn it to hell." I turned the cold water on, splashed it on my face with both hands, heard only that, then the water from the tap hitting against the porcelain of the sink. "Shit," I said again, and when I opened my eyes this time, I did not know anymore how I felt, except confused, all traces of the smile gone, any smile, and I stepped back from the mirror, then farther back, my reflection fading, departing, I thought, about to turn away without an answer, without a single clue, a stranger with a blank, white face, a ghost. "He has no advice for you," I whispered, and switched off the light and stood a few minutes longer in complete darkness. "This is where you've arrived," I said to myself, "after all this time, late afternoon, Christmas, 1965. Where to now? Europe? Another half-baked excursion to the East Coast? A one-nighter in the observatory? Where? For what? Too fast," I said. "Much too frigging fast. Step one is to sit back down and talk it all out. Move slowly, very, very slowly, whether she's impatient to leave or not. Play it safe and by your rules. Be sure what it is you want, and what it is you're doing. Okay? Go."

I pushed open the door, placed one foot in front of the other, and walked into the aisle. Except for the waitress making price changes on the menu, nobody was there. The cups had already been cleared from our booth, the tabletop wiped clean as though nobody had been sitting there. No note, no check, no tip. Outside I could see only Johnny's black pickup, the sky beyond beginning to darken, the streetlight already on.

I stopped at the cash register. "How much?" I asked, not even knowing if I meant for my coffee only or for both of them.

"It's taken care of," she said. "The girl paid."

Like always, I thought. Charge cards, allowance money,

interest from trusts and stocks. For years I had willingly let Phoebe cover the cost of everything—rent and food for the Northampton apartment and for eating out, for gas and long-distance phone calls, even for the deposit to hold a spot for me at Amherst College. She'd given me a car to drive, a key to her parents' house—the whole bit. Sponge, I thought, leech. No more. I'd get this one even if it meant paying twice.

"I want the bill," I said, taking my wallet from my back pocket. "I don't care if it's paid. I'm paying again."

She slid two fingers under the bill, lifted it slowly up the shiny spindle, handed it to me, and folded her arms. I thought, She stays open on Christmas, and her only two customers turn out to be cranks, fruitcakes.

"It's like this," I said, but I stopped. What the hell. There was no way to explain, no need. I handed her a dollar bill, and she rang up the sale, slid my change across the glass case, the boxes of cigars open underneath—El Productos and Garcia y Vegas and Phillies Cheroots. I walked all the way back to the booth, put down the tip. On my way out she said, "Here," and held out a small wicker basket, like a collection plate, heaped with candy canes, each one wrapped in its own clear plastic stocking of cellophane. I took two, not feeling I owed anybody a thing, and I said, "Thank you." I said, "Merry Christmas," and I buttoned my jacket and turned up the collar and stepped out into the cold.

I half expected to find a present from Phoebe on the seat of the pickup, and I was relieved when there wasn't one, just the half-empty bottle of Old Museum. I stashed it under the seat. Booze and advice. Don't drink too much, Johnny had said, but I had, though I felt perfectly sober now, the window open a crack, the radio on. I switched it off—I did not want to hear the cease-fire had been violated in Vietnam. I'd believe in peace, at least for this one day. That's how I felt, peaceful, knowing I'd done the right thing by dragging my feet in conversation with Phoebe, capitulating nothing, explaining only that I'd decided finally to attend the University of Michigan beginning second semester. Still, I wished she hadn't retreated like that. I wished we had at least said goodbye, and that bothered me more than I thought when I finally shifted into first gear and let out the clutch. I wasn't even sure what direction I should take out of the parking lot, toward home or toward Phoebe's. I didn't know until I edged the pickup's nose onto the country road and looked both ways.

It was that dangerous time of day, dull gray, almost no definition. But to the right I could see the Lincoln Continental, the exhaust streaming out white, the emergency flashers blinking. Phoebe pulled back onto the hardtop from the shoulder, slowed again, almost stopping, her hand out the window, signaling me to follow. I blinked my headlights, but they were pointed straight ahead, into a field of corn stubble. So I honked three times and I let her get halfway around the first bend before I swung left, the tires spitting gravel. I was glad she had waited, but I did not look behind. Instead I watched the clouds moving in, dark and thick, snow already slanting into the high beams. We had made some pair in the Bluebill, so perfectly mismatched, and I closed one eye, as though observing the arrangement of winter stars through the telescope, and I began to name them again, one star every minute, for as long as it would take to get home.